Why [...] when he'd had the chance?

"I'll go put in our lunch order. You can stay here and help Rori," his father said.

"No, Dad." If it were anyone else—anyone—he'd have done it before his father could volunteer him.

"Justin, you might as well go with your father." Rori spoke up, clearly not comfortable being left alone with the likes of him. "I can do it myself."

"That's not the way we do things, little lady. Justin, you can catch up with me at Clem's." Frank hopped in behind the wheel, looking pleased with himself.

He'd seen that mischief in his dad's eyes before. Playing matchmaker, was he? What, did he think that Rori, with her model good looks and college education, was going to take a shine to the same cowboy she hadn't wanted years before? Justin shook his head, vowing to give his dad a piece of his mind later.

"I'm really sorry about this." She did look sorry. Sorry about being forced to see him again.

That made two of them.

Books by Jillian Hart

Love Inspired

*Heaven's Touch
*Blessed Vows
*A Handful of Heaven
*A Soldier for Christmas
*Precious Blessings
*Every Kind of Heaven
*Everyday Blessings
*A McKaslin Homecoming
A Holiday to Remember
*Her Wedding Wish
*Her Perfect Man
Homefront Holiday
*A Soldier for Keeps
*Blind-Date Bride
†The Soldier's Holiday Vow
†The Rancher's Promise

Love Inspired Historical

*Homespun Bride
*High Country Bride
*In a Mother's Arms
  "Finally a Family"
**Gingham Bride

†The Granger Family Ranch
*The McKaslin Clan
**Buttons and Bobbins

JILLIAN HART

grew up on her family's homestead, where she raised cattle, rode horses and scribbled stories in her spare time. After earning her English degree from Whitman College, she worked in travel and advertising before selling her first novel. When Jillian isn't working on her next story, she can be found puttering in her rose garden, curled up with a good book or spending quiet evenings at home with her family.

JILLIAN HART

THE RANCHER'S PROMISE

Steeple
Hill®

Published by Steeple Hill Books™

STEEPLE HILL BOOKS

Steeple
Hill®

Recycling programs
for this product may
not exist in your area.

ISBN-13: 978-0-373-87601-3

THE RANCHER'S PROMISE

www.SteepleHill.com

Printed in U.S.A.

My voice You shall hear in the morning, O Lord;
in the morning I will direct it to You,
and I will look up.
—*Psalms* 5:3

Chapter One

"Justin, I finally got a call on the housekeeper job."

"Oh, yeah? That's a shock." Justin Granger hefted the feed sack, settling the fifty-pound weight easily onto his shoulder. As a rancher, he was used to heavy lifting and in his line of work, this wasn't considered heavy. He followed his dad out the open front door of the feed store, waved goodbye to Kit behind the counter and squinted in the hot late May sunshine. "I was beginning to think that putting an ad in the paper was a waste of time and money."

"I figure we got lucky. Not many folks want to cook for the likes of us." His dad, Frank Granger, swung two feed bags into the back of the white pickup parked curbside. "I made the interview for later today. If that doesn't fit your schedule, then I can interview the gal on my own."

"A gal?" That meant a woman. Not promising, not at all. Justin tossed the sack into the back and closed the tailgate. "I wish Aunt Opal hadn't gone to Arizona. She's about the only female I want to trust."

"Not all women are like Tia or your mom." Frank gave the keys a toss. "I'm sure there's one trustworthy gal around these parts, at least enough honest to cook three squares for us and wash our socks."

"You're more optimistic than me, Dad." Justin hopped behind the wheel and turned over the engine. Cool air breezed out of the vents, a relief from the intense summer heat that had hit hard and early. Not the best thing for the crops. They mostly ran cattle, but they grew their own alfalfa, corn and hay. "I don't see why Autumn and Addison can't do it."

"Hey, if you want to tell your sisters to do *house*work instead of ranch work, be my guest. I'm not touching that with a ten-foot pole. I'd rather wrestle a rattler bare-handed." Frank buckled up. "No, it's better we hire someone. I got a good feeling about this one."

"I hope you're right. I don't want to wind up with another closet drinker who falls asleep on the couch instead of fixing our supper." Justin checked the mirror. No traffic coming for as far as he could see, which wasn't a surprise. In a town the size of Wild Horse, Wyoming, it would have been a shock if there *had* been a car. He pulled onto the main drag, scowling. "If I remember, you had a good feeling about the drinker, too."

"Try to be more optimistic, son."

Justin rolled his eyes. Optimism was for birds and fools. He'd tried it once and hadn't liked it. He'd gotten his heart crushed and his illusions shattered because of it. In his view, it was wiser to expect the worst. Hard not to get disappointed or hurt that way.

"Looks like everyone's gettin' geared up for the festival." His dad sounded pretty glad about that.

"Guess so." Justin frowned, slowing down when the

mayor held up a hand and walked into the road. Wild Horse was a small town with a handful of necessary businesses and an equal number of others tottering on the edge of failure, like The Greasy Spoon, which had been The Brown Bag eight months before. Justin stopped, wondering what the mayor wanted.

"Mornin', Grangers." Tim Wisener strolled up to the passenger window. "Got some exciting news. Just heard it from my wife a few minutes ago."

"Don't tell me you're finally going to be a grand-daddy," Frank teased in his good-natured way. "Both your boys have been married for how long and no little ones?"

"Too long." Tim shook his head. "Don't know what it is with kids these days."

Personally, Justin got the Wisener sons' view of things. Facing the prospect of marrying a woman was tough enough—something he never wanted to do—but trusting one to raise a family in this remote, ranching town and stick with it when times got tough was a whole different question. He didn't want to wind up like his dad, raising a family and making a living when a wife kept trying to bail him. That was one drama he wanted to avoid.

"Martha sold the old River Lodge. Deal closes right quick. It's a lady from back east, New York, I think, putting down cash for the place and the cottage and acres behind it."

"That is good news. This town could use something besides one sorry motel. Too bad it won't be up and running for the annual shindig."

Justin didn't tune in to the older men's conversation. This couldn't have waited? He hadn't the time or incli-nation to worry about the old lodge. He had a ranch to run and time was wasting. Now he had a new woman to worry about. Personally, the family did need a cook, but he didn't have high expectations.

His dad kept talking, and Justin really didn't listen until his ears perked up at the mention of horses. Along with a fine herd of Herefords and Angus, they raised and sold working ranch horses. That was his sister's love. She possessed a knack for working with animals that no one in these parts had.

"Martha will be thrilled." Tim backed away from the truck. "I'll tell her to get a hold of Autumn."

"You do that, Tim. See you around."

Now that his dad was done jawing, Justin put the truck in gear. Something familiar caught his attention. He swung back to look at the woman walking along the sidewalk up ahead. She had dark blond hair with gold highlights, blue eyes the color of hyacinths, and his heart skipped three beats. He would know that heart-shaped face anywhere.

Rori. His high-school sweetheart. His palms went slick against the steering wheel. His pulse lurched to a shotgun start and galloped like a runaway horse. What was she doing back in town?

Not his business, he decided, whipped his gaze away and hit the gas. The truck zipped forward, but he didn't let his eyes stray from the single yellow line. He was over her, done with romance and emotions that took a man up and down and lower still. White-knuckled, he prayed she didn't notice them as they rolled by. Too bad he knew the sheriff was parked behind the library sign with radar, or he'd get up some speed and leave her behind in his dust. In fact, maybe a ticket would be worth it.

"Slow down, son." Frank buzzed open his window. "Rori! What are you doin' walking around town?"

Leave it to Dad, who had to chat with everyone. Tempted to keep on going, Justin bit the bullet and hit the brake. He could man up and face the girl who'd broken his heart, who had as good as told him he wasn't good enough for her. No need to let her know how that broke him. Back then he'd been too young to know a smart man didn't let a woman into his heart. All they did was cause wreckage and ruin.

Yep, he could handle this. He shoved the gear into Park and pulled the brake. Might as well get this over with. Let her see she didn't have an effect on him these days.

"Hi, Mr. Granger." She looked a mite surprised, folded a lock of silken hair behind her ear and approached the truck. Her gaze cut through the windshield and when she spotted him behind the wheel, she winced. The way her top teeth dug into her bottom lip, worrying it, was a clear sign. She wasn't comfortable seeing him either. "Justin."

"Rori." No need to sound overly friendly. Likely as not she was back in Wyoming only to visit for a few days. Probably attending Terri Baker's wedding. Had he thought it through and realized running into her might be a possibility, he would have stayed on the ranch and let his dad run the errands.

"Looks like you've got a problem, missy." Dad leaned out the window to get a good look at something. "Your horse threw a shoe."

"He's trying to. It's come off just enough that I can't ride him back to Gram's. I can't get it off, wouldn't you know?" She was a master of the shy grin. "I didn't think to bring a shoe-puller with me."

Don't get sucked in by that grin, Justin told himself. No way, no sir. He'd stopped being immune to her smile when she'd taken his heart, stomped it to bits and shoved it back at him. He opened his mouth to tell her they'd be happy to call her grandparents for her, but Dad unbuckled and opened the door.

"We got some tools. We can improvise." Frank's boots hit the blacktop. "Justin, get out here and help while I dig through the back, will ya?"

If it were anyone else—*anyone*—he'd have done it before his father could volunteer him. Justin's grip tightened on the steering wheel. Why hadn't he kept driving when he'd had the chance?

Gritting his teeth, he yanked the belt loose and tumbled into the road. With every step he took, he felt the weight of her gaze. He didn't like it, but there wasn't much help around on a Sunday afternoon. There was no one handy to take over the task of helping the lady in distress. Most of the businesses in town were closed and aside from the mayor out for a stroll, there wasn't a soul on the streets.

"I'll go put in our lunch order." Frank handed him a flathead screwdriver, a pair of pliers and a battered roll of duct tape. "You can stay here and help Rori."

"No, Dad." He couldn't believe his own father would do this to him.

"Justin, you might as well go with your father," Rori spoke up, clearly not comfortable being left alone with the likes of him. "I can do it myself."

"That's not the way we do things, little lady. Justin, you can catch up with me at Clem's." Frank hopped in behind the wheel and pulled the door shut, looking pleased with himself.

He'd seen that mischief in his dad's eyes before. Playing matchmaker, was he? What, did he think that

Rori with her model good looks and college education was going to take a shine to the same cowboy she hadn't wanted years before? Justin shook his head, vowing to give his dad a piece of his mind later. The pickup's engine revved and the vehicle took off, leaving him behind in the middle of town with the sun blazing and a hint of old anger beginning to brew.

"I'm really sorry about this." She did look sorry. Sorry about being forced to see him again.

That made two of them.

"Don't worry about it. This will only take a second." He stalked around her and approached Copper with an outstretched hand, palm up. "Hey there, old boy. Remember me?"

The gelding snorted, his tail swished and he nickered low in his throat.

"Guess you do." He stroked the horse's neck. "He's gone gray around the muzzle. He's gotta be what, twenty?"

"Twenty-one."

"Autumn's mare is getting up there, too." Justin's face softened as he stroked the horse again. "Looks like your grandfolks have been taking good care of him."

"He's happy on their farm. He rules the roost."

"At least that hasn't changed."

"Justin, you might as well hand over the tools and let me do this." She took a deep breath. Talk about awkward. Nothing could cover up the fact that she'd hurt him long ago, and the pinch around his dark eyes told her he well remembered. "I'll return your tools later."

"I don't mind." He looked as if he did. Tension corded in his neck as he ran one hand down Copper's back leg; his jaw went tight. A sure sign that he minded very much.

This was *so* not a good idea, especially when Copper

refused to lift his hoof. She knelt at Justin's side. Being near him felt strange. Enmity radiated from him like the sun's heat off the earth. She wished she could elbow him aside and take over. "I know how to remove a shoe," she insisted. "Let me do it."

"Still as stubborn as ever."

"Are you talking about me or the horse?"

"Hard to say. Right now the both of you are giving me a headache." His grin belied his words.

She touched Copper's pastern, and the gelding obliged by lifting his hoof.

"That's more like it." Justin fell silent, head bent as he edged the screwdriver beneath a bent nail head and gave it a good tap with the pliers.

It didn't look as if he was going to relinquish the job. She scooped up the roll of tape he'd left on the pavement. It was hard to believe after all this time she was face-to-face with him. What were the chances she would run into him on her first trip into town? And it wasn't fair. She hadn't been prepared. She hadn't been back for more than a few days, and here he was in real life—not a dream or a memory—his ruggedly handsome face as emotionless as granite.

Time had been good to him. The old affection she'd once felt was like a light going on in her battered heart. Not that she loved Justin—no, there was no chance of that now and he would never feel that way about her again.

So, maybe it wasn't old affection she felt. *Lord, let this be simply a touch of nostalgia.* At least, she could pray it was so.

She studied the rugged cut of Justin's profile, the shock of dark hair spilling over his forehead, the straight slope of his nose and the spare line of his lips. Familiar and dear, but time had changed him, too. It had matured his face, sculpted hollows into his cheeks and fine lines in the corners of his eyes. His shoulders had broadened, he was a man in his prime and looked every inch of it.

With a few yanks, he pulled the last nail out of Copper's hoof and the horseshoe clattered to the pavement.

He plucked the tape from her fingers without meeting her gaze. He tore off a few strips and expertly lined them along the edge of Copper's hoof, working quick but competently, still an accomplished ranchman. There was something about Justin's combination of down-to-earth country, stoic strength and capability she would always admire.

"That ought to get you two home. Just go slow. No galloping." He lowered Copper's hoof to the ground and retrieved the shoe. "Want me to put this in the saddle pack?"

"Sure." The wind gusted in a hot airless puff, stirring leaves in the aspens that marched down the sidewalks. A dust devil whirled a thick funnel in the feed store's lot, giving her an excuse to look down the main street. The sidewalks were as empty as the road. Way down at the far end of town, the distant sound of kids' voices rose from the drive-in, known for its selection of ice cream.

What did she say to him? He didn't seem concerned about the silence as he unbuckled the pack slung behind the saddle and slid the shoe into it.

"Grocery shopping?" His brow furrowed as he inspected the pack's contents. "Wouldn't it have been quicker to drive?"

Okay, this was even more awkward. She felt the weight of his gaze searching her face for signs. Maybe he was noticing the discount-store T-shirt, the denim shorts she wore and the inexpensive flip-flops on her feet. Knowing how small-town rumors went, he was probably curious where her luxury sports car was and her designer clothes. Maybe even her wedding ring.

Humiliation swept through her. Likely as not he was holding back an "I told you so." Maybe he was waiting to hear that the life she'd left Wyoming to find after graduation had not turned out better, just different. And the man who'd taken her to the opera and symphony hadn't compared to the one she'd left behind.

"I suppose you miss riding." He filled the silence without a hint of an "I told you so."

"Something like that." She lifted her chin, wiser these days and stronger than she ever could have guessed, even if her knees were wobbly when she went to untie Copper from the hitching post. "I haven't been in a saddle for so long, I almost forgot what to do."

"You didn't have a horse boarded somewhere in Dallas?" A hint of surprise dug into the corners of his mouth.

"No." Life was like that. She'd wanted a horse; Brad had said it would be an outrageous expense they couldn't afford. Things simply hadn't worked out. She knew God was in charge, taking her where He thought she should be. "Besides, I still have Copper. How about you? Still riding Scout?"

"Now and then. He's retired from ranch work these days."

"You must miss him."

"Work isn't the same without him. I didn't know you were coming back for Terri's wedding."

"Coming home was a last-minute decision." She gathered Copper's reins and drew him away from the post. It was easier to concentrate on rubbing his nose than on meeting Justin's gaze. She didn't want her old beau to know how wrong she'd been and how stupid. A country girl like her hadn't suspected Brad's duplicity until it was too late.

"Hope you have a nice stay in town." He tipped his hat, walking backward. A gentleman, for he could have vented his anger at her, he could have asked questions about her life she did not want to answer, things she did not want him to know. He could have brought up how she'd hurt him and that would have torn at her conscience, but he didn't. He squared his shoulders, nodded goodbye and ambled away, tools and tape in hand.

Lost chances. They troubled her as she slipped off her flip-flops and stowed them in the pack. You chose a path in life and you followed it. You never knew if it would take you where you wanted to go. You just had to trust, even if the choice had been a mistake. She never would have guessed the road she'd followed would have led her back home, full circle, standing right where she'd started.

Copper blew out his breath impatiently, as if to remind her that time was wasting. The sun bore down on her, and the blacktop sizzled beneath her feet. She swung into the saddle, ignoring the burn of hot leather, and reined Copper toward the edge of town.

At least *that* was over. Meeting Justin. Recovering from the shock of seeing him again. Her palms went damp, and it wasn't from the midday heat. She wished she could rewind, hit delete and replay the past few moments. She should have apologized to him. She should have asked how he'd been. She should have explained that the reason she'd come back wasn't only to attend Terri's wedding, although she had planned on going.

"I hadn't been prepared to see him so soon," she explained.

Copper shook his head, plodding along the strip of Main reserved for parking, a totally understanding friend. She rubbed her free hand along his warm neck, his coarse mane tickling the backs of her fingers. She'd been reconciled to the idea of seeing Justin later today at the ranch, where he would probably be busy in the fields. She hadn't been prepared to talk with him, to look him in the eyes and see how much bitterness had taken him over.

She still owed him an apology. She didn't intend to shirk from it. As a Wyoming girl, she knew how to stand up and take a hit on the chin.

The front door of the diner swung shut. A new neon blue and yellow sign proclaimed the establishment to be The Greasy Spoon, but everyone called it Clem's. Clem had initially run the place beginning with the First World War, when he'd bought the building new. He'd made the best milkshakes in the county. Bittersweet, she remembered sitting in a vinyl booth sipping on a shake and laughing with her high-school friends with Justin always at her side.

Was he thinking about those days, too? As Copper circled around the new white pickup parked along the curb, she kept her gaze glued on the empty road ahead. She didn't want Justin to think that she was looking for him through the sun-washed windows. The afternoon would prove to be tough enough without adding the memories of their old romance to the mix.

Chapter Two

Justin swiped the last two steak fries through the puddle of ketchup on his plate and jammed them into his mouth, already rising from the kitchen table. Eating takeout was getting old, especially since the town diner's menu variety was limited, but it was better than the alternative.

"Hey, not so fast, bud." His sister, Autumn, strawberry blonde and fragile-looking, unhooked her leg from the chair rung, snatched her tan Stetson from the sideboard and stole a wedge of pickle from his plate. "It's your turn to clean up."

"I'll do it after supper." He loped toward the back door and the mudroom, where his boots were waiting. "I've got fences to repair and a lupine patch I gotta spray."

"That can wait ten minutes. Dad, tell him, will you?" Autumn, two years younger and the bane of his existence when they were little, snagged a water bottle from the fridge. "If I'm stuck with a kitchen mess again, I'm going to chase you down, big brother, and rope you like a calf."

"Best listen to her, son." Frank glanced up from the

current issue of a cattleman's magazine. "I wouldn't mess with a woman when she's got that tone in her voice."

Autumn shot him a triumphant grin on her way out the door. "And wipe down the counters and the table, too. Use soapy water, not a wet paper towel. Or my threat stands."

An empty threat, but still. What was the world coming to? He had a good eight more hours of work to do for the day, and the Sunday-morning service and errands in town hadn't helped. "What we need is to lure Aunt Opal out of retirement with a huge raise."

"Not going to happen. Don't think I didn't try it." Frank slapped the magazine shut. "Might as well clean up. Got that interview in a few minutes."

"Great." Justin stuck his head in the mudroom to give Autumn a few instructions on the yearlings, but she was already outside. Determined to catch her, he hit the screen door, sending it flying against the wall with a bang.

A horse neighed in protest, he heard a woman's "whoa!" and a thud of something hitting the dry dirt. A dust plume rose, shielding the rider who had taken a fall. Justin shrank a few inches, recognizing the red gelding skittish in the driveway.

Copper.

A tall, willowy figure rose up, at first a slim feminine shadow in the dust, but as the cloud began to settle, details emerged. The things about Rori he would never forget—the swirl of her long straight hair in the Wyoming breeze, the curve of her porcelain-cut chin, and the way she looked classy even wearing a battered baseball cap.

"What are you doing here?" He heard the venom in his words and winced. He hadn't meant to sound harsh.

His thoughts had somehow influenced his voice, the same unexplainable way he had found himself mysteriously on the edge of the lawn without realizing he'd moved a single inch off the porch.

"I'm falling off my horse, apparently." She dusted herself off. "Copper still doesn't like loud sudden sounds."

"If you're out of practice riding, then you are out of practice falling." There were a couple of dried blades of grasses stuck in her hair and a streak of dirt on the hem of her shorts. "Hurting anywhere?"

"I'm tougher than I look." She smiled, but it didn't reach her soulful eyes. He didn't know what her life had been like in Dallas, but the bright sparkle that used to light her up was gone.

"Howdy again, Rori." Frank's voice behind him was deep with amusement. "If your grandfather wasn't able to replace that shoe for you, I can take Copper to the barn and get it done."

"Really? I don't want to put you to any trouble."

"Me? No trouble for me. I didn't say *I* would do it."

Yep, leave it to Dad. Not that he wouldn't have made the same offer, but his old man didn't have to sound so pleased about it. "I'll take the horse. Go back inside and finish your lunch, Dad."

But did Frank listen? No. "You and Rori go on inside and get settled. I'll be back to start the interview in a few."

"Interview?" His brain screeched to a stop. He meant to set out after his father to take the horse and get Copper shoed, but his boots mysteriously stuck to the lawn. Rooted in place, he tried to shake the fog out of his head. He couldn't have heard that right. "Interview?"

"For the housekeeping position." Frank tossed over his shoulder as he took the reins from Rori. "Don't let his bark trouble you none. Justin's gotten cranky over the years. We manage to put up with him because he's family."

"I'm sure that's the only reason." Her laugh was like a trill of a creek, bubbling, quiet and inviting, leaving him thirsting to hear more. Unaware of her effect on him, she shoved a stray strand of hair beneath her baseball cap. "Thanks, Mr. Granger."

"If you're gonna be working for me, you've got to call me Frank." He clucked to the gelding, who followed him confidently, and the two set off down the gravel and dirt road to the horse barn.

"Thanks, Frank," Rori called out with a smile, earning a wave as man and horse turned the corner and disappeared from sight. She faced him, looking a little pale. "I guess you didn't know I wanted the job?"

"Would I be standing here with my jaw dropped if I did?" He jammed his hands in his jeans pockets, mostly wanting something to do with them. Throttling his dad didn't seem like a good idea, and it certainly wouldn't solve his problems with Rori. "Why didn't you say something in town?"

"I thought you knew."

"If you're looking for work, then that means you're staying around and this is not a quick trip home for Terri's wedding." Anger unrooted his feet and he marched toward the house. "You lied."

"No, I *am* going to Terri's wedding. I assumed your dad told you that I was here for an extended stay."

"Dad didn't tell me anything." Nothing unusual about that. He could guess at what his father was up to.

The wind gusted as if it were in cahoots with his dad because it brought the faint whiff of Rori's rose-scented perfume. He strode the same path they used to walk hand-in-hand. He marched up the back porch and ignored the swing where they'd spent many a summer afternoon sipping homemade lemonade and doing their homework.

Judging by Rori's silence, she might be remembering, too.

"Maybe I should ask. Do you want me to apply for the job? I understand if you don't." She swept past the screen door he held for her and waltzed into the mudroom like she'd done hundreds of times a dozen years ago. "The thing is that I need a job, and there aren't many positions available in town. Nothing else, as a matter of fact. That's the only reason I answered your dad's ad."

"Sure, I get it." He let the door slam shut and followed her into the kitchen, boots and all. "I suppose that fancy lawyer you married will be following you soon. Will he be putting up a shingle in town?"

"No. Brad won't be coming. I'm on my own." Raw emotion cut across her face and while she set her chin, straightened her shoulders and visibly wrestled it down, her sorrow remained. Sadness that was banked but unmistakably bleak in her violet-blue eyes.

Sympathy eked into him, and he did his best to stop it. No need to feel sorry for the girl who'd gotten everything she wanted. He yanked the refrigerator door open. "Sorry it didn't work out."

"Me, too."

He set his heart against her. He was no longer swayed by her emotions. He felt sorry for her. A failed marriage was nothing to celebrate. But that was as far as he was willing to go. He plunked the pitcher onto the table and went to fetch a glass out of the cupboards. He ought to say something more to fill the silence, but anything he could think to say would make him seem interested in her life.

Hardly. She'd made her decision, and now he made his. She might be thinking she'd settle for her second choice. After all, he was still available, right? Oh, he knew how women thought. They were largely a mystery, but he'd learned a thing or two over the years. The bottom line with them was wanting security, marriage and a man to pay the bills. The bigger the man's wallet, the better.

He slammed the glasses onto the table with enough force that the clunk reported through the kitchen like a gunshot. He glanced down, surprised that he hadn't broken them. That was when he realized half of the table was free of foam containers, plastic bags and the plates from lunch. "What do you think you're doing?"

"Clearing a place so we can talk about the job." Rori calmly set the armful she'd gathered onto the nearest counter, studied him with her steady gaze and backed toward the door. "But now that I see what you really think, I'm going to go. I thought we were adults and what we had was water under the bridge, but I was wrong. I'm sorry, Justin. I really am."

Uh-oh. His scars were showing, wounds he'd vowed to keep hidden and buried. He hung his head. "Didn't mean to growl at you."

"It's okay. I know you well. Your bark is worse than your bite."

"I never bite."

"I'm glad that hasn't changed." She gripped the screen door handle.

"You don't need to go."

"Are you trying to tell me that you wouldn't mind me working here?" She'd been the one to leave. She'd broken his heart. That she was here at all showed how desperate she was. She didn't need to read minds to know what he was debating. She opened the door, fighting to hide her disappointment. "I don't blame you. I understand."

"No, wait. Give a fellow the chance to think." He paced after her, squinting at the sunlight when he joined her on the porch. "I haven't had time to prepare myself for seeing you again. I need to think this through. You, the interview, it was all sprung on me."

"I suppose that was your dad's plan." She could see that now. Frank had been downright cheerful on the phone when she'd first called. He'd been welcoming earlier that morning in town. And now he'd set them up in the kitchen together. He wanted to give them time alone. Frank had meant well, but this wasn't what she wanted or Justin, either, judging by the frown carved into his granite features. There was nothing else to do but to leave. She eased down the steps and into the burn of the sun. "Your dad is destined to be disappointed."

"I think I heard the front door shut." Justin cocked his head, listening. "Suppose he's sneaking in through the living room listening in to see if his plan is working?"

"I can't believe he would do this. Your dad is not a romantic."

"He always liked you, Rori. He said you were good for me."

"You were good for me. You were a great boyfriend. I'll always be grateful for that. We grew up together."

"Up and away." He hadn't forgotten. His face was set, his emotions stone. But had he forgiven?

She didn't think that was likely. She didn't blame him. She'd been overwhelmed when he, the quarterback of the football team, had asked her, a freshman, to go to Clem's after school for shakes. For as long as she had been able to remember, she'd had a crush on Justin Granger. Three years older, he'd been every girl's wish—smart, kind, strong, funny, popular and drop-dead gorgeous. There had only been one thing she'd wanted more in life than being Justin Granger's girl—a college education and the chance to study music.

"So, are you back to stay? Or is this a temporary thing?" Justin's deep voice hid any shades of emotion. Was he fishing for information or was he finally about to say, "I told you so?"

"I will probably go back to teaching in Dallas when fall quarter starts, but things could change. I'll just have to wait and see." The things in life she used to think were so important no longer mattered. Standing on her own two feet, building a life for herself, healing her wounds—that meant everything now.

God had given her no other option but to return to her grandparents' tiny house for the summer. She had to think He had a purpose in bringing her here. One of her favorite verses was from Jeremiah. *For I know the thoughts that I think toward you, says the Lord, thoughts of peace and not of evil, to give you a future and a hope.*

"And this man you married?" he asked. "Did he leave you, or did you leave him?"

"He threw me out." She adjusted her baseball cap brim and waited for Justin's reaction. Surely a man with that severe a frown on his face was about to take delight in the irony. She'd turned down Justin's love, and her husband of five years had thrown away hers. If she were Justin, she would want her off his land.

"You were nothing but honest with me back then."

He leaned against the railing, the wind raking his dark hair, and a different emotion passed across his hard countenance. "I was the one who never listened. I loved you so much back then, I don't think I could hear anything but what I wanted."

"I loved you, too. I wish I could have been different for you." Helpless, she took another step toward the driveway. She didn't know how to thank him. He could be treating her a whole lot worse right now, and she would deserve it. "Goodbye, Justin."

"I suppose you need a job?" he called out from the railing, casually concerned.

"I'll figure out something." Needed a job? No, she was frantic for one.

How did she tell him the truth? That she'd been given enough money for a bus ride home. That she'd never thought twice about letting her husband handle the money, or the fact that he'd cleaned out the bank accounts and cancelled her cards before he'd replaced her with his plastic-surgery-enhanced receptionist.

"I haven't had a chance to get that shoe back on Copper," he called out.

"Gramps can do it tonight." Probably. If not, she could always call in the farrier. Costly, but it had to be done.

"Tell you what? You stay and round us up some decent supper, and I'll take care of your horse." Justin loped down the steps, his long-legged stride eating up the distance between them. "That will be the interview. If the food is edible, then as far as I'm concerned the job is yours. It's really up to my dad."

"Really?"

"I'll hardly be around most of the summer anyway. You know how it is. Long hours on the range."

"You're agreeing because you've figured it out, haven't you?"

"Discount-store clothes a size too large—probably your grandmother's. Am I right?"

Rori ignored the sting of her pride. The plain yellow T-shirt was Gram's, something the older woman had never worn much, and so were the flip-flops. "I didn't have a whole lot of time to pack."

"You don't have a car, do you?" Justin stalked closer. "That's why you rode Copper over here. No clothes, no vehicle and no money. That's my guess."

Shame scorched her face. She scrambled to hold on to her dignity. "I really don't feel comfortable discussing this with you."

"That fancy big-city fellow you married left you without a care." Anger dug into the corners of his mouth, making his high cheekbones appear like merciless slashes beneath his sun-browned skin. "You didn't deserve that."

"That's not what I expected from you." She stared at the grass at her feet to avoid the pity in Justin's eyes— pity for her. She couldn't blame her circumstances on anyone but herself. No pity needed. What she had to do was to wise up. Reach inside and find the tough, country girl she'd once known.

"Why don't we let the past stay where it belongs? Behind us." Justin hiked backward toward the barn. "It's gone. Done and over with. We'll just go on from here."

"Employer and employee, you mean?"

"That's it." He gave her a slow grin, the one that used to make her heartbeat flutter in adoration.

Maybe there was a tiny hint of a flutter—just old memories, nothing more as she watched him go. Looked as if she had a chance for this job after all. With any luck, there would be enough groceries in the pantry to whip up a supper the Grangers weren't likely to forget.

She hurried back to the house, glad to find Justin's dad holding a box of recipe cards left behind by his aunt Opal. It was nice to have some inside help.

"Is that Copper?" Autumn skidded to a stop in front of the corner stall. "Did Mr. Cornell bring him over?"

"Nope." Justin circled around her in the barn's main aisle, hefting his working horse's saddle. "Rori rode him over."

"Rori? You mean she's in town?"

"No need to look so excited about it." He'd done his best not to think about her all afternoon long. His work was tough and demanded all of his attention, but somehow she'd remained at the front of his mind. Patching up a calf, checking on his herd, hauling feed and playing vet, all the while bothered by the image of Rori Cornell in a hand-me-down shirt and sadness deepening her violet eyes.

He mentally hammered up a barricade around his heart. Sure, he might feel sorry for her. She'd obviously come on hard times. But that was all he intended to feel for her. Ever.

"She's up at the main house." He shouldered through the tack-room door and plopped the saddle onto a saw-horse. He would wipe down the leather this evening. Not that he was in a hurry, but he knew if he didn't show up for supper, Dad would come out looking for him.

Frank had always thought the world of Rori. Probably because she had always been honest from the get-go. She'd always had bigger plans than settling down in small-town Wyoming. He figured she was always meant for something better.

"I can't believe it! Rori came back for the wedding, didn't she?" Autumn deposited her saddle, dancing in place. "I can't believe no one told me. Then again, considering the men around here, maybe I can."

"I can feel your gaze boring a hole in the back of my head." He gave Copper a nose rub on his way outside. "I'm not the reason she didn't call up and tell you she was back in town. Don't blame this on me."

"Who else?" Autumn padded after him. "Besides, that's what big brothers are good for. Taking the blame."

"Funny." He rolled his eyes. "And before you say it, I'm over Rori. It doesn't matter to me that she's here."

"There was a time when I would have called you a liar if you'd said that, but now I know it's true." Autumn caught up with him, the heels of her riding boots crunching in the grass. A sign of her determination. "You've become a cold, hard man, Justin. I'm worried about you."

"Nothing new there." He'd been like this a long time. It had taken him a while to learn the important lessons about women, but he'd finally done it. "No need to worry about me. Go on up to the house and catch up with your old friend."

"*My* old friend?" Autumn sounded as if she was going to correct him but then decided better of it. "Aren't you coming, too?"

"Got a mare I need to check on first." He climbed through the board fence into a grassy paddock. A small band of expecting mares looked up from their grazing and wheeled in his direction. "I won't be long."

"Need any help?"

His sister stood there, the sun at her back, the only

female he could count on. She did a man's work without complaint day in and day out come blizzard cold or blistering heat and still he couldn't trust her with the truth.

Help? He would need a ten-gallon bucket of it if Rori ended up working for the family. Yet how could he object? She wouldn't have left behind the city life she'd chosen if she had any other option. He wanted to keep his distance, but that didn't mean he wanted to see her hurting.

God had a way of keeping a man humble. Justin tipped his hat brim lower to keep the sun off his face, held his hands out to show the mares he'd come without treats and went on with his work.

Chapter Three

"Mighty fine grub, Rori." Mr. Granger—Frank—dug his spoon into the big bowl of chili in front of him. "We haven't eaten this good in months."

Judging by the look of satisfaction on his face, he was telling the truth instead of tempering it with kindness. Relieved, she turned back to the sink. She wasn't the most accomplished cook, since she and Brad had employed a maid who'd done most of the food preparation. "I've gotten rusty, but being home with Gram and Gramps has given me some practice."

"If this is rusty, I can't wait to eat what you fix when you're back in practice. Autumn, where did Justin get off to?"

"He had to check on a mare."

"He missed grace, and if he's not careful he's going to miss supper." He didn't look all that happy with his son. Probably it was disappointing work being a matchmaker.

"Do you want me to stick around, or should I take off?" She'd tidied the kitchen and put all the prep dishes into the dishwasher. "I can stay, but my grandparents—"

"Are expecting you." Frank nodded. "Sure, go ahead. It's Justin's turn to do dishes, since he left the lunch mess."

"Serves him right," littlest sister Addison piped up from her side of the table. It was hard to get used to her being so grown up. When Rori left town, Addison had been eight. Now she had just finished her junior year of college. The girl with the ponytails and freckles was only a memory replaced by a tall beauty. Addison frowned, wrinkling her perfect complexion. "Justin looks down on kitchen work."

"He does, and it's our job to keep him in line," Autumn added with a wink.

What Rori wanted to do was to get out of the house before Justin walked in. Not that she felt compelled to avoid him, but her dignity was bruised. He pitied her. No doubt, that wouldn't change. She grabbed her ball cap from the hat hooks by the back door. "Thanks. Have a good evening, everyone."

She slipped outside listening to the three Grangers at the table call out their goodbyes to her. The sunlight had tempered, the blazing heat kicked down a notch to hint at a beautiful early summer evening. She hopped down the steps and hurried across the lawn, the grass fragrant beneath her flip-flops.

The hills, the stretch of the high prairie and the rim of the breathtaking Tetons in the distance surrounded her. She trudged toward the barn, keeping a lookout for Justin. Best to avoid him if she could. That wouldn't always be possible now that Frank had offered her the job, but it was likely. Justin had changed, and she hated to think she had played a hand in that.

What I would give to go back and do it over again, she thought, half prayer, half impossible wish. If she could turn back time, she never would have accepted his offer for their first fateful milkshake together. She would never have trusted or married Brad.

"Rori!"

She heard the wind carry her name. Through the lush green fields she saw Justin in the knee-high grasses, his hat shading his face and a gloved hand raised up to her. More than distance separated them. She waved back, hurrying to the barn, and freed Copper from a stall. The white-muzzled gelding nickered a warm welcome and pressed his face in her hands with unmistakable affection.

Warmth filled her—emotions she'd been battling since she'd come home. Copper's steadfast friendship, the sweet-scented grass and the earthy hint of dust in the air, the endless blue skies, it all overwhelmed her. Life may have led her away but her roots remained deep in this land. The days of long ago felt so close she could almost hear them. The sound of the radio in Dad's truck, running up the back steps to the whir of Mama's mixer in the kitchen, the carefree head toss Copper used to greet her with when he was young, bounding up to the fence.

"I missed you, too, old buddy." She leaned her forehead to his, her best friend. "C'mon. Let's ride home."

By the time she'd saddled and bridled him and mounted up, the yard was empty of all signs of Justin. He was probably inside finishing up the chili and cornbread she'd made. Maybe he was seated at the table and facing the windows overlooking the backyard and the mountain view.

Was he watching her now? she wondered as she reined Copper toward the driveway. Or was he doing his best to avoid her? She sat straight in the saddle, glad when the curving road took her out of sight. It was sad how much had changed between them, when they had once been so close.

Of course, that was her fault, plain and simple. She drew her cap brim over her eyes and, squinting into the light, rode the low rays of the sun home.

"How is Wildflower?"

Autumn's question came from as if far away. Justin shoveled a steaming spoonful of chili into his mouth, hardly feeling the burn on his tongue. He grabbed a nearby glass, gulped down some milk to put out the fire, and realized everyone in the kitchen was staring at him. Addison struggled to hide a grin.

"Seems he's got something important on his mind, girls." Frank, grabbing a cookie from the stash they'd bought from Clem's, couldn't look happier. "Looks like Autumn had better ask her question again."

Justin cleared his throat. He was in no mood for ribbing, however well-intentioned. "Wildflower is fine. She's close to her time."

"Too bad Cheyenne isn't back from school yet. I reckon she'd like to be there when her mare foals." Frank grabbed his root beer off the table. "The Mariners are on. Anyone going to join me?"

"I will." Addison bounded up from the table, still coltish and energetic, her strawberry-blond ponytail bobbing. "Are you comin', Autumn?"

"No, I'm going to go sit with the mares and leave Justin with the dishes." His oldest little sister seemed pretty pleased with herself, too. "Have fun, brother dearest. I know what you think of housework."

"I don't have a bad opinion about housework," he argued. He had more outside work than he could get done in a day, the last thing he needed was more. "I just don't want to do it."

"Sure. We wouldn't want you to demean yourself," Addison joked.

"Not our brother." Grinning at him, Autumn stole her Stetson off the wall hook. "I don't know how you turned out to be so grumpy. You must have gotten a bad gene. It's a shame, really."

"A terrible shame," Addison agreed from the counter, where she was helping herself to a cookie. "Is it my imagination, or is he grumpier tonight?"

"He's definitely grumpier," Autumn agreed. "Let's hope his mood improves."

"Or it's going to be a long summer," Addison predicted, backing out of the room to join their dad. The TV droned to life in the next room.

"It will be a longer summer if you two don't knock it off." He scowled over another spoonful of chili. "Or else."

"Yeah, like we're scared." Autumn plopped her hat onto her head. "You're all bark, Justin."

"You never know. One day I might change."

"I'm not worried." She stole a cookie from the counter, too. "I've known you all my life. You're one of the good guys."

"Yeah? Haven't you heard? Good guys finish last."

"You're thinking of Rori?" She nibbled on the edge of the cookie. "What happened to her? She looks so sad. Is there something I should know? Her grandparents are all right, aren't they?"

"Rori didn't say Del and Polly were having health problems."

"Just checking." Autumn said nothing more, waiting a beat before she padded through the door, but what she hadn't said lingered more loudly than if she'd uttered the words.

Rori wasn't all right. She was hurting. Regardless of what he'd come to think about her and women like her, he didn't like that. Not at all.

Blurry-eyed, Rori bounded through the early morning kitchen, eyes glued to the coffeemaker in the corner. Thank heavens it was chugging away. The smell of caffeine lured her straight to the counter.

"Good mornin', Pumpkin." Gram's voice startled her. There was a clang of a pot at the stove. "Aren't you up early?"

"This isn't early. This is still technically nighttime." Dawn was a light haze at the rim of the dark world. "Do you get up every morning like this?"

"Early to bed, early to rise."

"That's your secret to being healthy and wise." She grabbed a cup from the cabinet. "I'm going to ride Copper over to the Grangers and leave you and Gramps with the truck."

"Oh, we were looking forward to running you over there." Gram flipped sausage links in the fry pan. "Del is so pleased to have you back, he's over the moon. I am, too. Your sweet face livens up our place."

"Not as much as yours does." She brushed a kiss against her grandmother's cheek. "I won't be home until late."

"Should I keep a plate of supper warm for you?"

"No, but leave the dishes. I have to make myself useful some way." The sound of coffee pouring and the fragrant smell of the rising steam made her sigh. A few jolts of caffeine and maybe her brain would stop feeling heavy and foggy. She hadn't slept so hard in ages. It was all the fresh air and country living. At least being forced to come back home had a few perks.

"You know I can't let dishes sit around in the sink. Goodness." Gram laughed to herself. "The idea."

"Try it, would you?" Rori slid the carafe back onto the burner and reached for the sugar bowl. "I have to earn my keep, and I'll be mad if you don't."

"I don't want you mad." Gram slid a sausage from the pan onto a paper-toweled plate. "I want you stayin' around as long as you can."

"Me, too." Rori gave the coffee a stir and set the spoon in the sink. "There's no place like home."

"You remember that when you start thinking about leaving us at summer's end." Tears prickled in her grandmother's gentle blue eyes. "Not that I blame you, but I miss you and your sister when you're not around."

"Ditto." Rori squeezed her grandmother's frail shoulder, unable to say how hard it had been to stay away. Visits home weren't enough, and a part of her had been sorely missing. She loved her work at the private arts school where she taught piano and music theory, but it took coming home to remember how much she loved Wyoming's peace and quiet, the restful stretch of rolling fields, hills and endless sky of this farm and the family she loved. Her grandparents had taken her in and her younger sister when their parents had been killed in a blizzard. "Give me a call if you need anything. I won't be home until near dark."

"Have a good day, Pumpkin." Gran whipped open the oven door and wrapped something in a paper towel. "Here. You need breakfast."

She took the scrambled egg-white sandwich with thanks and headed outside. Things were simple here.

Balanced meals three times a day, no endless hurrying, no pressure to measure up, no feeling like a Wyoming girl out of place in her husband's life.

It was an odd feeling to grab the jingling bridle from the barn, whistle to Copper in the pasture and slip between the barbed-wire fencing as she did when she was younger. If only she could take an eraser and wipe away that chunk of time she'd spent in Dallas, then maybe she could find a way to be happy again. Erase her mistakes and find some peace. Wouldn't that be a blessing?

"Good morning, old friend." She petted Copper's nose when he came up to her. She laughed when he tried to get a hold of her sandwich. "That's not for you. Sorry."

Copper gave her a sheepish look, as if he were saying he had to give it a try anyway. She slipped the bridle over his head, the bit into his mouth, and managed to get onto his back without spilling her coffee. They headed off through the fields surrounded by birdsong and the golden crown of the rising sun. Beauty surrounded her. The only shadow that loomed ahead of her was thoughts of Justin.

He wanted to leave the past behind them. Water under the bridge. He apparently had no problem doing that. He had probably gotten over her in a flash. Men were built that way, she feared. They didn't feel as deeply as women did. Love didn't rope them in as much, nor did it sink beyond the heart to the soul.

Justin had gotten hurt when she'd told him she couldn't marry him and set aside her dreams for him. But he probably hadn't shed a tear over it. He probably didn't feel racked with regret regardless of the number of years that had passed. He just probably turned off his heart like a switch, and she was sorry for that.

He would never know how much she had wanted to

say yes. She took a bite of her sandwich and a sip of coffee. He would never know how afraid she'd been of living a life without having reached her biggest goals, ending up with nothing but a list of regrets. Losing her mom in junior high had affected her forever. Life was finite. You had to make it count.

Ironically, she'd racked up more regrets by running toward her future. One thing was for sure, there would be only smart decisions and careful choices from here on out. As if in agreement, the sun peeked over the rolling hills, bringing light to the shadows.

Justin heard the muffled clip of horseshoes on the hard-packed dirt outside the main horse barn. He stuck his head over the rail to see Rori riding in on a sunbeam. Dust motes danced in the soft yellow rays, hazing her like a dream.

Or, he realized, like an answer to a quick prayer. Wildflower was standing next to him, skin flicking, head down, panting heavily. "Rori, can I ask you to race up to the house and call the vet?"

"What's wrong?"

"My sister's horse is having some trouble." He kept his voice calm and authoritative, letting the mare know he was confident and in charge of her. That was the best way to comfort the frightened creature. "The number's on the wall above the kitchen phone. Tell Nate it's Wildflower and he needs to get over here pronto. Oh, and fetch my dad, too."

"You got it." She wheeled the red horse around and with a touch of her heels, the gelding leaped into an all-out gallop. Head down, tail flying. It was good to see the old gelding still had his racing legs.

Wildflower blew out her breath to get his attention. She watched him with unblinking liquid brown eyes, staring so hard it was as if she were trying to give him an important message. Good thing he spoke horse.

"I hear you, girl." He rubbed her muzzle. "Let's try to walk you. Are you game?"

She followed him into the aisle, head down, winded. First foals could be tough on a small mare. He and his dad had kept a close eye on her and they'd caught her trouble as early as they could, but she had a hard row ahead. He wished Cheyenne had been able to make it back home from vet school. He could really use her help right now. He didn't want to be the one she blamed if things went wrong.

"Just keep it slow and steady, girl. I'm right here with you." He and Wildflower had made it to the end of the aisle and carefully turned around before hooves drummed outside. Rori rode up, dismounting in a graceful sweep. She was a welcome sight, as hard as that was to admit. "Did you reach Nate?" he asked her.

"I heard him running to his truck before he hung up on me. He promised to break speed limits on the way over." She patted Copper's neck and led him into the end stall she'd used yesterday. "Your dad said he's on his way, too."

"You're a lifesaver. Of all the mornings to forget my cell phone."

"It's hard to function properly before sunup." She unbuckled the old bridle and gated the horse in. "She's not looking so good. Is there anything I can do to help?"

"We'll see. If she holds off until the vet gets here, then you are free and clear. But if not, I'll need your help with the foaling."

"Okay." She reached over the rail to grab the empty

water bucket from Copper's stall. "I'll fetch some water first, and then take over walking her if you want to get the stall ready."

"I'll take you up on that. Here." He ambled close and stole the bucket from her grip.

This close, she could smell the hay on his T-shirt and the soap from his morning shower. Without a hat, his dark hair stood up on end, still shower damp, and his lean cheeks were freshly shaven, showing off the deep groves bracketing both sides of his mouth, groves that transformed into dimples when he grinned but now they were grim set lines.

"Thanks ahead of time." He put distance between them. "It's good to have you here after all."

"Oh, you say that as if it had been a huge question? I thought we settled that."

"I know. I might not have been fully truthful yesterday. What I *want* to feel and what I admit to feeling are two different things." He handed over Wildflower's lead. "This is the truth. When I saw you ride through that door, I knew I could count on you."

"Back at you." She clucked to the mare, encouraging her forward. "The vet is going to be here in a bit. Your dad is coming. She's going to be just fine."

"As long as we can get that foal turned first, she will be." Grim, determined, he hiked to the nearby sink. The walled-off room hid him from her sight, but nothing could diminish his steady, capable iron will and his endless decency.

It was heartening to know some things didn't change. That for all the prickly layers and cool granite Justin had become, he was still underneath the cowboy she'd always admired. His heart wasn't switched off completely, after all. She may as well face the fact that she would probably always be just a little bit in love with him.

She cooed soothingly to the struggling mare as they took slow painful steps down the aisle.

Chapter Four

Justin upended the bucket into the stall, letting fresh grain tumble into the feeding trough. The polite old gelding nickered what sounded like thanks and swished his tail before nosing in to lap up the treats. One animal cared for. He knuckled back his hat, watching Rori out of the corner of his eye. The bulk of his thoughts ought to be centered on the expecting mare, but his mind seemed drawn magnetically to the woman, fresh-faced and so wholesome she made his teeth ache.

She looked as if she belonged here with her light hair tied back in a single ponytail swinging slightly with her slow gait. The concern for the mare touching her face made her a hundred times more beautiful than any makeup artist could. With the sun spearing through the skylights above and through the open doors, she looked ethereal, too lovely to be true, and something straight out of his forgotten dreams.

Footsteps padded through the grass and dirt. Dad's gait, dragging a bit from a long night spent up and down checking on the mares. Frank came into sight. "Looks like she surprised you."

"Yep. I came out to feed the stock and Wildflower was down in the field."

"I wasn't talking about the horse."

Justin frowned. Impossible to miss the grin on his dad's face. He figured he would set them up, was that it? He shook his head at his dad. Now wasn't the time to hash this out. The horse was the concern. His boots carried him down the aisle and before he realized it he was at Rori's side, doing his best not to notice the light spray of freckles on her nose as he took the lead rope from her. As careful as he was, his fingers brushed hers. Her skin was warm and satin-soft, and a shoot of tenderness took root in his chest.

"You can go on up to the house now." His voice sounded scratchy and thick with feelings best left unexamined. "Thanks for your help."

"Any time." She stepped away, shy and graceful as always, as if nothing significant had happened between them. Of course she hadn't reacted to his accidental touch. Why would she? She backed down the aisle, glancing between him and his dad. "Call me if you need anything. I'll be back with some coffee."

"Bless you." Frank tipped his hat to her. "I could use some chow, too."

"I'll see what I can do." She ran her hand gently along Wildflower's swollen side. "It's going to be okay, girl."

Don't start liking her again, Justin told himself. He'd always been a sucker for a woman who was kind to animals. That's what had gotten him noticing her in high school in the first place. A few years ago, that's why he'd decided to trust Tia.

"Same old Rori." Frank ambled close and rubbed the mare's neck. "Good to see that it's true."

"What's true?" He turned his shoulder, afraid that his dad had noticed something Justin wasn't ready to admit to himself.

"You can take the girl out of the country, but you can't take the country out of the girl." Frank smiled as he spoke, as if he was greatly amused. "Why, what did you think I was going to say?"

"Let's just help the mare." His face heated. He didn't like that his dad *had* figured things out. Just because he liked Rori didn't mean a thing. Probably he always would like her. She was a nice woman. "Think we can wait for the vet?"

"Get Wildflower in the stall, and I'll scrub up." Frank gave the horse another caring pat, for the mare had nickered at the sound of her name. "It won't be much longer now, sweetheart. You go with Justin."

"Dad, you know nothing is going to happen between Rori and me, don't you?" He gently eased the mare toward the birthing stall.

"Is that what you think?" A barrel laugh rang out as he disappeared into the washroom.

"Isn't that why you have been trying to push me and Rori together?" Fresh hay crinkled beneath his boots and Wildflower's hooves.

"I figured the two of you ought to resolve things. It's not good to leave loose ends the way you have with that gal." Water rushed, pouring into a stainless-steel sink. "Don't you reckon it's time you forgave her?"

"For running out on me?"

"For doing what she had to do. For following the path the Good Lord set her on." The water cut off, and Frank ambled into sight, drying his hands and forearms on a fluffy blue towel. He tossed it over the top of an empty stall gate. "You're not so good at forgiveness, son."

"I don't want to be you. No offense." Wildflower lowered her head, heaving, her knees buckling.

"Let's get her on her side." Frank jumped to help. He had worked with animals all of his life, and it showed in the skill and comfort his touch seemed to bring Wildflower. The mare leaned her neck into his hands.

One day he wanted to be as good a man as his dad. The trouble was, he didn't want to be as gullible. Their mom had left Dad twice. Both times Dad had wrestled with a shattered heart, later accepted her apologies and let her back into their lives. Then he'd taken care of her when liver disease set in.

No one in their right mind would ever call Frank Granger a fool, but he did have a big heart. Too big.

That was something Justin would make sure he would never have. No way did he intend to let any woman tread on his dignity like Dad had allowed Mom to. At the time, Dad had young kids who missed their mom and wanted her back, too, but a man could only take so much. Justin had already reached that limit.

"Sounds like Nate's here." Frank stopped to listen. "Yep, tires in the gravel. Help has arrived."

Justin ran his hand down the mare's nose, murmuring low to comfort her, and forced his thoughts away from Rori.

But it didn't work.

"Need a hand?" Autumn swaggered through the mudroom and popped her head into the kitchen.

"No, I'm managing just fine." Rori slapped the last

omelet onto the last plate and turned off the burner. "How is Wildflower?"

"A brand-new mama." There was a *thunk, thunk,* presumably Autumn kicking off her boots before she strode into the room with two large thermoses. "She made it through just fine once they got things heading out straight. She has the cutest little filly. All long legs, bottlebrush mane and the biggest brown eyes. Cheyenne is going to flip when she gets home."

"Glad there's good news. I could tell your dad was worried. He was totally frowning. I didn't know he was capable of it." She rescued the platter of bacon and sausage patties from the warm oven and walked down the counter, filling plates. "I'll get you all some more coffee and tea in a jiffy. I was going to bring breakfast out to the barn."

"Sounds like a good idea. Dad was up half the night checking on the mare as it is, and you know Justin, grumbling about being behind with the morning chores." Autumn set the thermoses on the counter and rolled her eyes. Her light auburn hair tumbled loose around her shoulders. At first glance, no one would peg her as a tomboy, not with her china-doll complexion, deep hazel eyes and leggy stature, but Rori knew no one could outride her. She'd tried many times. "How is Bella?"

"Still the best horse in the history of the world." Autumn uncapped the thermoses. "I had to stop and say hi to Copper. He's looking good for his age. Your grandfather is pampering him."

"Gramps can't help himself. Once a horse lover, always a horse lover."

"That's the truth. It's the way God made us." Autumn yanked the coffee carafe from the machine and upended it over a thermos. "It has to be weird being back. You've been away for so long."

"I hadn't realized how much I've missed this pokey little town. Not one thing happens there." She did her best not to remember the past and the impatient girl she'd been. And how eager to experience something more exciting than dinky Wild Horse, Wyoming. "It used to drive me crazy, but I'm thankful for it now. It's reassuring when home always stays the same."

"Speaking of things that haven't changed. Clem's— now The Greasy Spoon—still makes the best burgers around." Autumn screwed the cap on the thermos and reached for the hot-water carafe. "Have any plans, say, middle of the week?"

"Are you thinking horse ride?"

"Just like old times." There was a quiet question hanging in the air between them, but Autumn didn't ask it. Instead she finished pouring the water. "I'll run this outside. Need me to take anything?"

"How about the muffins?" The sausage platter was empty and she set it aside to snatch the cloth-covered basket from the edge of the kitchen table.

"Yum. Smells good." Autumn hugged the thermoses and took the basket into the crook of her arm. "Hate to rain on your parade, but guess who's listening at the door?"

"I'm not listening," a man grumbled from the mud-room. "I'm getting some clean towels for the barn."

Justin. Rori's palms went damp, and she wiped them on her jeans. Great. Why hadn't she noticed he was there? How much had he overheard?

"Yeah, right." Autumn chuckled as she strolled out the door. "You could have asked me to bring back the towels."

"Didn't think of it." Justin sounded easygoing as

he spoke with his sister. "Did anyone think to call Cheyenne?"

"I'll do it," Autumn called out a split second before the screen door slapped shut.

Rori set the plates on a tray she'd found in one of the bottom cupboards and covered the steaming food. With every movement she made, she was infinitely aware of Justin in the next room, the faint shuffle of his boots on the tile floor, the muted squeak of a cabinet door closing and the rustle of fabric as he paced to the kitchen door.

"Need any help?" Hard to tell if he was being friendly or just helpful, as he might be to any hired hand.

"Nope, but thanks. I've got it."

"You could make us trudge into the kitchen to eat, you know. You don't have to bring food to us."

"I don't mind. You've all had a busy morning and it's not even six o'clock." She opened the drawer and began counting out flatware. This is just conversation, she told herself. Justin had meant what he said about letting bygones be. He was making an effort, and it mattered. She could, too. "Since you're standing there with a free hand, you could grab the juice on the counter."

"Good. I like to make myself useful." A faint hint of his dimples carved into either side of his mouth. He ambled into the kitchen, shrinking the room with his size and presence. He casually scooped up the pitcher and the stacked plastic glasses without complaint. "You need to come see the new filly."

"Autumn said she was the cutest thing."

"Foals usually are." He held the door for her, and somehow the morning seemed brighter as they headed down the steps and along the path together. "You were calm under pressure, Rori. You helped a lot."

"I did nothing. I called the vet. I walked the horse." She shrugged. "Anyone could have done the same."

"Not anyone. I was afraid you had turned into a city slicker, but I can see you've still got some Wyoming girl in you. I'm glad you're working here. It's a big responsibility running this place, and it will be a burden off Dad's mind to know he's got someone in the house he can rely on. Someone to feed us and the hired men when we get hungry."

"I'm glad you think I'm a help." She held the tray steady, flatware and dishes clattering with each step, and squinted against the low slant of the morning sun. She'd forgotten her ball cap. Grass slapped against her shins, crunched beneath her shoes and barely hid a jackrabbit who startled away into the field as they approached.

"Rori." Frank hurried out of the barn to take the heavy tray from her and shot his son a telling glance. "That's too heavy for you to carry all this way."

"No problem. I'm stronger than I look."

"Oh, the problem wasn't with you. I thought I raised my son better than that."

"I offered, but she turned me down." Justin put the pitcher and cups down on top of a barrel.

"I did. I wouldn't have given up the tray if he'd tried to wrestle it away from me." She followed Mr. Granger and the tray to a walled-off room next to the tack room, where a sink and counter, microwave and small refrigerator sat as neat and as clean as any kitchen. A small battered dinette set huddled in the center of the area. Frank slid the tray onto the faded pink Formica top and the rest of the Grangers plus the vet descended on the table.

"Want to come see her?" Justin's voice rang low, but

even with the clang of dishes, rise of voices and cheerful conversation it was the only thing she heard.

"I'd love to." She floated after him, excitement tingling through her. It had been ages since she'd seen a newborn foal. She loped down the aisle, the stalls empty this time of year, and felt the fingers of the past trying to grab hold of her. She was at home with the warm scent of horseflesh and grain in the air and the concrete beneath her feet. Maybe she'd never realized how much she loved country life.

"Hey, there, Wildflower." Tender-toned, Justin knelt down at the stall bars. "We just want to get a good look at your baby."

"Your beautiful baby," Rori corrected, wrapping her hand around the rail and kneeling beside him. Wildflower nickered low in her throat, a proud mama who turned to lick at her little filly's dainty ear.

Nothing could be sweeter than the little gold-and-white bundle curled up in the soft clean hay. The newborn stared at them with a surprised expression, as if she didn't know what to think about the strange faces staring in at her. She blinked her long eyelashes and stretched toward them as far as her neck would allow.

"That's a pretty girl," Justin soothed, holding out his hand, palm up, his motions slow.

The filly gave his fingers a swipe with her tongue and drew back, as if her own boldness startled her. Wildflower nickered gently to her baby and, as if encouraged, the little one's head bobbed down as she scrambled to get up on her spindly legs and point them in the correct direction.

Sunshine tumbled through the open top half of the stall door, gleaming on the mare and foal's velvet coats.

Wildflower rubbed her chin on her daughter's shoulder, a congratulatory pat, and nickered proudly. The tiny filly wobbled on her thin, impossibly long legs and flicked her bob of a tail joyfully. She took a few proud steps. Her front knees gave out and she landed in the soft hay.

"Poor baby." Rori reached through the rails instinctively, making sure the newborn was all right. The foal looked up at her with big, wondrous eyes, and Rori felt her chest catch. Hard not to fall in love with the wee one. She couldn't help brushing her fingers across the soft velvet nose. "You will get the hang of it. I promise. Keep at it."

The foal's eyes drifted shut, as if she liked the gentle stroke.

"You still have a way with animals." Justin's low voice moved her like the brush of the summer air and the peace of the morning. Familiar, and it was what she'd missed over the years.

"I do all right." She didn't have a gift, just love for creatures large and small. "Not the way you do."

"I got it all from my dad." No way to hide the affection in his voice. "I learned a lot growing up at his knee. One day, I might be good enough to take over the place when he retires."

"Word is that he's cutting back, handing over a lot of the responsibilities of the ranch to you and Autumn."

"Your gramps was talking about me, huh?" He paused as the filly opened her eyes, set her chin with determination and positioned her front hooves for another go at walking. "Dad wants to retire, but truth is, he loves the work. It's not like he has anything else to do. He's single, and he's done raising all of us."

"It's good that you're close. You must spend a lot of time with him."

"A perk of the job." He'd sacrificed a lot for his dad and for this ranch that had been in his family for five generations. "It's what I like most about ranching. Long hours in the saddle talking with my dad."

"I can't picture you doing anything else but ranching." She gazed up at him with those big blue eyes.

He felt the impact like a touch to his cheek. Her gaze raked him, as if she were trying to see past the titanium barrier he'd put up.

"You still love the work," she stated, not questioning. That's how well she knew him.

"Truth is, I would have liked a lot of things, but this is what I chose." He paused as the filly pulled herself up and swayed, but what he was seeing was Rori. The changes in her—more mature and seasoned and longing for something he couldn't name. "Truth is, after you left town I couldn't take it. I missed you so much."

"You missed me? But you said—"

"That I wouldn't even notice if you were gone?" he repeated his horrible words, angry at himself for saying what could never be taken back. She didn't even understand what she'd been to him. "No one knew I applied to college and got in. A late admission for the winter quarter in agriculture sciences at Washington State University."

"Where I was." Her hand covered his, warm and comforting, a connection he did not break.

"I was all set to accept when Dad took a bullet. Rustlers. They got away with about a thousand head of cattle. I was too busy trying to save my father to stop them."

"I'd heard he was hit. I remember Gram and Gramps talking about it. I called several times, but no one was home. I didn't feel right about leaving a message. When I heard he was all right, I didn't call again."

"It was touch and go for a while there. We almost lost him. I ended up staying and pulling my weight around here, so Dad could recover. The bullet nicked his heart, so there was no question. He had to take it easy to heal right."

"You're a good son to him, Justin. A good man."

"Looks can be deceiving." He grinned, fighting the moment, because the way she peered up at him made him feel ten feet tall, the way he used to feel when she loved him.

Careful, knowing he needed to put the brakes on his thoughts, he extricated his hand from hers a little too quick and rough. Her face fell as if he'd slapped her, but he couldn't help it. The tenderness that had taken root in his chest ached, tenderness he had no right to feel, and he'd better figure out a way to pluck it right out. It would not be wise to have gentle feelings for Rori. When summer ended, she would be out of here. Wild Horse, Wyoming, was too small for her—*that* hadn't changed.

"Look at her go!" Dad's warm chuckle broke the moment, filling the silence that had fallen and chasing away the hurt look on Rori's beautiful face.

Justin tried to force his attention to the filly awkwardly loping the length of the stall. She skidded to an unsteady stop, swaying. She shook her head, flicked her tail and gave a little bleat of happiness. Victory.

"Cheyenne's gonna be sorry she missed this." Frank shook his head, moseying over to the rails. "Watch, she'll probably drive up this morning. What are you two doing here? Catching up?"

"Admiring the foal." Rori seemed to know what his dad was up to and wasn't intimidated one bit. "You are going to have to hold your horses, sir, because your matchmaking efforts are not going to work."

"Wasn't trying to matchmake. But since you put it that way, are you sure there isn't a chance?"

"Dad." Justin rolled his eyes, shook his head and counted his blessings. He wouldn't trade his father for anything, but he would like the right to keep a few things private. Judging by the knowing look on his father's face, Frank wasn't fooled. They both knew that what Justin felt for Rori wasn't gone—not by a long shot. Trying to be friendly with her wasn't working. Time for a new plan.

"I'd best get my breakfast and hit the range." He turned tail on Rori, determined to follow the path his life had taken and one he would not change—a path that led away from her. He didn't look back.

Chapter Five

Justin. She couldn't forget the warm moment between them or the way he'd jerked from her touch as if she had the plague. Not even prayer had helped. It was not easy to get him out of her mind when signs of him were everywhere she turned. There was his coffee cup with his name on it that she had rinsed and fit into the dishwasher's top rack. Blue towels she harvested from the dryer to fold, which had his name monogrammed on them. When she went upstairs to put them away, she was bombarded with the images of him in framed pictures marching up the walls of the stairwell. Justin as a baby, Justin as a toddler, Justin as a little boy.

I never should have taken his hand like that. She shook her head, wishing she had kept the urge to comfort him to herself. What had she been thinking? She hadn't, that's what. She'd reached out to him instinctively, as she would have done to anyone who was talking of something painful, but the way he'd jerked away from her had felt like a slap. Worse, it felt like a rejection.

After you left I missed you so much. His confession in

the barn stayed with her, lodged like a knife too deep to pull out. Obliterating everything she'd believed about him. Why hadn't he told her? She'd never known how he felt. He'd always kept his most intimate feelings private.

It looked to her as if he were still doing the same.

His room was spare and neat with no clutter on his nightstand or dresser. His bed was made, his blinds open to the panoramic Teton range. She set the pile of towels on the foot of his bed and continued on her delivery. When she was leaving a stack of brown towels on Mr. Granger's bathroom counter, the phone rang.

She dragged the empty laundry basket behind her as she raced the length of the hall, skipped down the stairs and plucked the cordless handset from the cradle.

"Hello? The Granger residence." She set the basket on the floor next to the kitchen counter.

"Uh, I'm looking for Stowaway Ranch?" A woman's pleasant voice hesitated across the line.

"You have the right place. How can I help you?"

"I'm looking to buy a horse, and the mayor's wife gave me this number. I need to speak with Autumn, please."

"If you don't mind holding, I'll be happy to check for you."

"Thank you so much." Her voice was polished-sounding, with a slight East Coast accent.

Curious. Rori hit hold on the multiline system and frowned at the radio. It had been a while since she'd used a two-way. She assumed it was on the right station as she unhooked the mouthpiece and hit the call button twice. "Justin?"

No reply. The dishwasher gurgled, the only sound in the silent kitchen. The window over the sink showed a sunny vista of sprawling meadows and a distant rising hillside. A bright white speck sat midway up the slope. Justin was working in the field, hopefully not too far from his truck. She clicked again. "Justin?"

"It's Frank. What's up?" The radio squawked.

"I've got a call for Autumn."

"Hold on, I'll go fetch her."

While she waited, she tried not to read too much into the fact that Justin hadn't answered her call. Chances were that Frank had been closer to the truck. That Justin was tangled up repairing a fence or busy feeding grain and it was easier for his dad to grab the radio. That was all.

If only the image of him striding away from her would amble straight out of her mind, along with the look on his face when he'd yanked his hand out from beneath hers. It wasn't quite terror or disdain, but it had been close.

"Rori? It's Autumn. What's up?" She sounded breathless, as if she'd been working hard and had run to the truck.

"I got a call for you." After she'd followed Autumn's instructions for patching the caller through to the barn, she hauled the basket back to the laundry room.

As she stuffed washed clothes into the dryer, she tried planning her shopping list for town, but her thoughts returned to Justin. He'd applied to college? She couldn't believe it. Justin, at college? She tried to imagine him living in a dorm, hauling a backpack jammed with books across campus and spending his time studying.

No way. Whenever she thought of him, she couldn't place him anywhere but right here on Granger land.

She grabbed the hundred-dollar bill Frank had tucked beneath a set of truck keys for her use, scribbled out a list and headed out the door. The instant her sneakers touched the top step, her gaze arrowed to the rise ahead, where Justin's white pickup was parked along the fence line.

Regret. It grew with every step she took, and it wasn't the only emotion haunting her. The old feeling she'd tried to explain away as nostalgia, as a fondness for what had been between them, trailed her to the garage. Even out of sight, a piece of her heart longed for him.

Lord, what do I do? She wasn't over Justin at all.

He wiped the sweat from his brow and watched the tan pickup amble down the driveway. Brake lights flashed through the growing dust cloud slowly stealing her from sight. If he were given to poetic notions, he would say he lost a chunk of his heart as she left. Good thing he wasn't prone to such nonsense.

"Son, are you going to daydream or grab the other end of the board?" His dad cut into his thoughts.

Justin shook his head, realizing how things must look, him staring after her like a love-struck fool. He grabbed his water bottle, took a healthy swig and went down on one knee. So his dad wouldn't jump to conclusions, he ground out with what he hoped was enough bitterness, "Did you *have* to hire Rori? Of all the women in the county?"

"She was the only one who answered the ad. What did you want me to do?" Frank hefted his end of the board, fit it in place and hauled his hammer out of his belt. "Besides, she needs the job. She looks down on her luck."

"No comment, Dad. I don't want to talk about her."

"You two were looking pretty cozy in the barn earlier." A few whacks of the hammer and Frank drove nails deep into the fence board. "I thought you two had a chance to clear the air. Maybe work out your differences."

"What's there to work out? She left, now she's back. It has nothing to do with me." That would be his new plan—indifference, distance and diversion. He drove a few nails into the post and hooked his hammer into his belt. "You didn't think I was still in love with her, did you?"

"No." Frank's denial rang with humor. "But a dad can hold out hope, can't he?"

"Don't tell me this has anything to do with talking with the mayor yesterday. Grandkids were mentioned. Remember?" He yanked his saddlebag off the ground and swung it over his shoulder. "You need to stop with the matchmaking."

"I admit to no such thing." The twinkle in his eye was a guilty one. "And even if I was, Rori was good for you, son. You can't hold what she did against you."

"She didn't want me." His work horse was grazing. He gathered Max's reins and swung the leather pack behind the saddle. "I proposed and she said no."

"If I remember right, she said for you to ask her again after she graduated from college."

"The same difference." Justin heard the growl in his tone and regretted it. Swinging up into the saddle gave him time to rein in his turmoil. "You're trying to polish up the past and put a pretty bow on it. It won't work."

"I didn't say it was perfect. What do you think, Scotty?"

Their hired hand Scotty, who had been on the ranch for as long as Justin could remember, looked up from packing his tools. "I say you're both wrong."

"Not me," Justin denied. Wrong? He wasn't going to stay and listen to this. His pride bruised, he eased Max through the tall wild grasses. "But I agree with you about Dad."

"Hey, now maybe I am wrong, maybe I'm not, but

you're wound up pretty tight." Frank mounted up, not one to be left behind. "Don't you understand what happened?"

"I don't want to rehash this. I can't go back. I learned that from you always going back to Mom."

"The past will always be chasin' you unless you come to terms with it. *That's* what I hope you learned." He pressed Rogue to a trot. "Something tells me you missed the lesson."

"Not now, Dad."

"Now's as good of a time as any." He caught up to his boy and slowed his horse to a walk. Side by side, it was easy to get a good read on the boy. His oldest son, his firstborn, was the one most like him in temperament. He remembered not being much different at the same age, which seemed a lifetime ago. He'd been a husband and father trying to wrangle both jobs on top of making a living off this land. He'd been stretched thin, and he hated to admit it, just as prideful as Justin.

What would have happened if he had learned his lessons earlier? The lessons about pride and defensiveness, understanding and forgiveness may not have made a difference in his marriage. Lainie had her own set of problems. But those lessons might have made a tough go a little easier on everyone.

"Believe me," he told his son. "There will come a time when your pride isn't as important as other things. A time when you wish you made things right with the girl when you had a chance."

"I know what I'm doing, Dad."

"Yes, that's just what I said when I was your age." From the ridge he could see the faint dust smudge and the blot of the beige pickup as Rori turned onto the main road to town. It took two to make a marriage work, but it only took one to make it fail. He'd learned that the hard way, too. Relationships could tear the heart out of a man. "I want you to make peace with the girl, that's all. Whatever you think, I want you to be happy."

"I am." Chin up, shoulders straight, iron strength, that was his boy. "At least, I'm as happy as I'm going to be."

Stubborn. A chip off the old block, Frank mused. As he rode the crest of the hillside, the breeze rustled through grass and trees, the plod of the horses' gaits added a muted percussion to a glorious day. His fields rolled over hillsides and stretched along flatland for as far as he could see. A pair of eagles wheeled overhead in perfect synchrony and a jackrabbit darted ahead of the horses, leaping to safety, and stopped to take a look at the coming procession. The creature wrinkled his nose, eyes curious as they rode by. Up ahead a pasture of horses grazed in the sunshine, and in another cattle lounged in the shade.

Yes, he was a blessed man. He spotted another problem with the fence. Looked as if the bull had been kicking the fence again. He drew Rogue to a halt.

"Dad!" Autumn's call broke the relative stillness. She galloped in with a smile on her pretty face. To him she would always be the little girl with a ponytail and freckles, Daddy's girl. "I think I've finally found the right buyer for Misty, or as much as I could tell over the phone. We'll see next week when she drops by."

"Good." Autumn looked pretty happy. That always perked him up. He dropped Rogue's reins, swung down and hauled his saddle pack with him. The woman who had bought the lodge, he remembered from his talk with the mayor. Autumn had a gift with horses, and he liked to see her venture as a trainer taking off. He hefted his tools to the ground. "Tim said she'll be renovating the cottage behind the lodge, too. Could be she might need boarding for a while, before she gets some of that acreage fenced off."

"I'll be sure and talk to her about that. I'm psyched." Autumn dismounted, as pleased as punch. "What's with Justin? He looks like he sat on a bee."

"To my way of thinkin', he always looks like that." With hammer in hand, Frank gave the board a wrench, neatly removing a bent nail. When Justin protested, they all laughed until even he joined in.

Yes, Frank thought, he was richly blessed. Life was a tough battle for everyone, this he knew for certain, but there were so many parts of it that were worth the fight. This moment was one of them.

His daughter hiked over to help him replace the board, his son went to work on resetting the far post. The flawless blue sky above made him feel as if God were watching over all of them. Maybe there was a lot more good waiting on the road ahead for his family.

Encouraged, Frank swiped the sweat from his brow, grabbed a few new nails and bent to his work. The ringing of hammers filled the air.

Was Justin really going to stay out there? Rori squinted through the darkening glass, the kitchen window offering her a fair view of the stubborn man.

He'd climbed into the corral with the expecting mares, and in the falling twilight they gathered around him with tails swishing and noses outstretched, beautiful horse-shaped shadows ringing a solitary man. With his Stetson, wide straight shoulders and cowboy's stance dark against the last fiery remnants of sunset, he could have been a scene from a movie come to life. Justin had always been a larger-than-life hero to her.

Didn't they say first love never died? As she dried her hands, the scent of dish soap on her skin tickled her nose. She had to admit this was true in her case. Old pieces of the love she once had for him were like dying embers she thought had gone out. But once stirred again, they gleamed with a light of their own.

She hung the towel on the oven handle so it could dry, her movements echoing in the lonely kitchen. Boot steps rapped up the steps and the screen door whispered open. A man's gait, but not Justin's. She could still see him out of the corner of her eye. The man who could be cold as steel was also gentle, his stance softer, his head bowed, his hands peaceful as he stroked one mare's neck and then another. The real Justin Granger revealed.

"It's gettin' late, missy." Justin's dad ambled into the room. "You put in a long day, longer than I wanted for you."

"There was a lot to do. I've got the main floor of the house spic and span." She gestured toward the cookie jar. "A batch of snickerdoodles made."

"My favorite. You know how to make the boss happy, that's for sure." When Frank smiled, it was contagious. Rori found herself grinning, too, as he lumbered over to the counter. He lifted the top of the porcelain cow-shaped jar. "I don't want you feeling as if you have to compensate because of Justin."

"He doesn't like that I'm here."

"Darlin', it isn't what you think. He's been like that since the day he proposed to you." Frank bit into one of the two cookies he'd taken. "This is one great cookie. You did well today. This kitchen has never looked so good. Now get home, see your grandfolks and unwind. And don't let Justin worry you none."

"I'll try."

"No trying. Just do." Frank winked as he ambled away. A few moments later the TV's faint drone murmured from the living room. Sounded as if he was catching a sports show.

Time to go. She grabbed her baseball cap and burst out into the temperate night. A very forward cow leaned over a nearby fence and bawled at her, puppy-dog eyes bright with friendliness. Crickets sang in the grasses and a handful of deer looked up from grazing, their soft eyes watchful as she headed toward the barn. The path led her straight past the field with Justin and the horses. She didn't see him at first. The mares spotted her and several of the beautiful animals loped straight up to her, pressing their barrels against the white board fence and reaching their noses as far over as they could.

"I know, I smell like cookies." It was why she'd stayed late. Justin hadn't come in for dinner, and she wanted to wait for him. But he'd been exceptionally busy, considering the rest of his family and ranch hands had come in for the evening meal hours ago.

One horse nickered. Another whinnied. A white mare shook her head, as if demanding the cookies she could scent.

"Headin' home?" Justin's abrupt question rose out of the half dark, a disembodied voice that startled her.

"Yes. I suppose you're glad to be rid of me for the day." She meant the words to be light, but the man emerging out of the shadows did not smile.

"Dad seemed happier today knowing you were taking care of things at the house." He sounded gruff, a mix of anger and something colder. "It means a lot that you're here. For however long that lasts."

She squinted at him, not quite believing her eyes or her ears. He could have been a stranger. Had Justin really changed that much? Where was the gentler man she'd spotted among the mares? "Do you mean to do that?"

"Do what?"

"To compliment me for being here and then hit me with an insult."

"I only meant you might not realize it, but folks are counting on you. Not me, but my sister. My dad." His shoulders squared like a man ready for a fight.

Well, he wasn't going to get one. She could read him even in the shadows. She didn't need to see his features or to be able to see the emotion playing in his eyes to know he hurt every bit as much as she did. The past felt alive and the gap between them as wide and vast as the Grand Tetons. She could see the spearing peaks behind him, black against the encroaching night, dividing the past from the present moment. She wished she could forget that long-ago, flawless time when the two of them had been in love.

"Good night, Justin." She turned on her heel. The mares wrangled for her attention but she couldn't pet them without being near to Justin. She would not let him pull her back into their old conflict. She kept walking. "I left your supper warming in the oven."

"Don't do me any favors, Rori. I don't need them."

She swallowed hard, perhaps to keep down a gasp of shock. He sounded harder than ever, like a man who'd lost more than his heart. Maybe her working here was costing both of them more than she'd anticipated.

Bad decision, she realized as she hurried up the lane.

But she hadn't had another choice. She needed to work. It was a puzzle why on earth the good Lord had brought her to the Granger ranch. She felt raw inside, wrung-out and worn. By the time she reached the barn, she realized Copper was tied in the aisle, saddled and ready to go.

Justin's work, no doubt, and his statement couldn't be clearer. Pain wrapped around her like a shroud, heavy on an evening rife with Wyoming beauty. She snuggled her horse, mounted up and didn't look back as she reined him into the meadows. She felt Justin's gaze as harsh as a hand to her spine pushing her from his sight. Stars winked to life and a warm breeze serenaded the trees, but not even the beauty of God's handiwork could lift the ache from her soul.

He watched her from the back steps, where the shadows behind the house were darkest. He had a good view of her astride Copper, riding tall and willowy. She'd always been a beautiful sight whether it was in the saddle with the wind in her hair or standing in the twilight looking ready to put him in his place.

He wished he could forget the hurt he'd put on her face. He'd been too harsh tonight, that was for sure. He raked a hand through his hair, feeling defeated. He'd only been trying to be proactive and protect his vulnerabilities. If he didn't put up his defenses, then she would waltz right in and wrap him around her little finger all over again.

He couldn't go through that brand of torment again. She'd brought him to his knees because he'd made the mistake of loving her so much.

He lifted his head, his gaze zeroing in on her instantly. He felt her presence in the dark, for he didn't need eyes to see. The night had claimed her, and she was only a hint of movement, a faint glimpse of an outline. Distance was stealing her from him, even the small beauty of looking at her, the only part of her he could allow himself to have.

Watch over her, Lord. He sent the prayer heavenward, just as he'd done every night since she'd left town years ago. Over time, she had become his only true prayer.

When he was sure she'd safely crested the hill, he climbed to his feet. The deer close to the house looked up from their grazing, watchful and unafraid as he reached inside the door. His fingers closed on a cool metal handle of the scoop he kept inside the mudroom door. Full to the brim with grain he carried it to the edge of the lawn where he dumped it, talking low to the creatures.

The pampered pet cows in the closest pasture began to bawl, begging for similar attention. The deer kept their space as he circled around them, giving them plenty of leeway, and handed over the last treats to the cows. Buttercup rubbed her nose against his hand, begging for a little petting. Usually he would oblige her but tonight he felt restless. He heard the house phone ring, the musical tones spurred him to action. He ran to answer it. No doubt it was Cheyenne calling to report in on her long drive home from Washington State. It took all his might to banish Rori from his mind.

Chapter Six

"I've noticed things haven't been going so great between you and Justin." Autumn dunked a golden steak fry into a puddle of tartar sauce. "What can I say? Sorry doesn't seem to cut it. There's no excuse for my brother."

"So it's true." Rori sat up straight on the faded red vinyl seat. "Justin *has* been avoiding me."

"Big-time."

Their booth at Clem's was in the back alongside the window, giving her a perfect view of the entire restaurant and the street, where Copper and Autumn's first horse, Bella, waited at the hitching post in the building's shade. Rori dipped a fry through the pool of ketchup on her plate, processing Autumn's confession. "I wanted to think he was just busy out in the fields. When I do see him, he's heading in the opposite direction. Every time."

"Like when you brought lunch out to the west quarter section today?" Autumn nodded, reaching for another fry. "He couldn't move fast enough. His lunch was cold by the time he came back and Dad had eaten half of his sandwich. Served him right."

"Maybe tomorrow I had better bring extra, just in case. He's bound to take off again."

"Sure. He'll suddenly remember something he needs to check on about the time he spots you riding up the hill." Autumn smiled. "I could calf-rope him, hobble him and force him to stay, but that's a little extreme. I promised Dad I wouldn't rope any of my brothers unless it was really, really necessary."

Rori burst out laughing. She couldn't help it. It was good to be home with her childhood friends. "Autumn, I've missed your sense of humor."

"Oh, you think I was joking? It's a threat I just might use one day. Brothers." She shook her head, scattering light auburn hair over her shoulders. "It wasn't easy growing up stuck in the middle of those two."

"I remember." She spooned a mouthful of strawberry milkshake out of the enormous glass. It was too thick to drink with a straw until more of the ice cream had melted. She knew that Tucker had moved off the ranch, looking to get out of the small town, too. "You were always trying to keep up with Justin and outdo Tucker. Look where it got you. Working alongside your dad and training your own horses."

"I do okay." Autumn shrugged, staring far off down the street as if lost for a moment in thought. "Not too many men in these parts are interested in a woman who can outride, outrope and outshoot them."

"All you need is one man. The right one."

"Finding him is the tricky part. Then when you think he's the right one, he always disappoints you."

"Tell me about it." Rori nodded in sympathy. The wounds of her failed marriage were still too raw to think about. "Or the right man isn't right for you."

"Justin's coming."

"What?" She nearly dropped her spoon. The icy concoction on her tongue hit the roof of her mouth—brain freeze. She blinked against the pain, her eyes blurring slightly so Justin strode into sight on the sidewalk looking as if he was riding on the slanting sunbeams.

"Oh, he hasn't spotted you yet. But look, he just noticed Copper." Autumn propped her chin on her fist, as if watching a particularly interesting part in a favorite movie. "Watch the panic spread across his face. He's stopped in his tracks. Now he's staring at the horse as if he's debating. Should he proceed or turn tail and run?"

"If he wants to avoid me, then let him." Maybe Justin was right. Maybe this was easier. The sun-glazed glass made the scene ethereal, like something out of a dream, like the past come full circle. She saw the handsome man with her schoolgirl's heart, the Justin she'd always loved—his strength, his goodness, his open laughter. How his voice would only drop a note when he spoke to her. Only to her. How special he'd made her feel, how safe and loved.

She'd been sure he would wait for her. Sure he would understand. But he hadn't loved her enough. And having that happen twice in her life was too much. Maybe she was meant to be alone. Maybe this was what Justin felt, too, whenever he looked at her.

He'd changed so much.

He must have sensed her because he pivoted on his boot heels, his gaze finding hers through the window. She could not get over how remote he looked, as if he were carved of marble. Only a muscle ticking in his jaw gave him away.

"I'm going to go pay." Autumn grabbed the ticket off the edge of the table, holding up one hand prepared for a protest. "This is my treat for old times' sake."

She wanted to argue, but she knew what her friend was up to. "Thanks, Autumn."

When she turned back to the window, Justin had turned away, strolling out of sight, retracing his steps.

Message received, she thought, refusing to let her head hang. Amazing. His rejection hurt as much as it had done twelve years ago.

Lord, help me to handle this the right way. She pulled a decent tip out of her pocket, tossed the bills on the table and took both milkshake glasses with her.

"I'll get that." Sierra Baker in her checkered apron met her at the counter. She had two paper cups in hand and a friendly smile. Sierra might have been a few years behind Rori in school, but they'd been friends in the church's young life program. "It's good to see you, Rori. Terri is over the moon that you're going to be at the wedding."

"She has three days to go until the big day. How is she doing?" Rori handed over the milkshakes, grateful for the interruption.

Forget about Justin, she told herself. Let him go.

"It's crazy." Sierra transferred the milkshakes into the cups. "The usual last-minute things are falling through. The favors haven't arrived. Tom's mother is refusing to come. The church hall had a water heater break and the carpet is still wet. Let's face it, weddings are nerve-racking. Mine was no different."

"Or mine." Her stomach twisted at the thought. Hers hadn't been the wedding of her dreams mainly because of the horrible feeling she couldn't get rid of. That through the years when she dreamed of her future wedding, Justin Granger had always been the groom she wished for, the only man she'd wanted waiting for her at the end of a church aisle. The end of that dream was a wound that faded with time, but did it end?

No, her heart answered. After all this time, after everything she'd been through, that dream remained within her, something treasured that had been lost and found again. She wished she could stop it, but she couldn't.

"Maybe Terri will have her happily-ever-after. The good Lord knows that didn't happen for me." Sierra snapped lids on the cups and pulled two paper-coated straws from her apron pocket. No ring marked her left hand.

Sympathy swept through her, aware of the pain of a failed love and how deep it went. "I'm sorry, Sierra."

"You, too?" Sierra handed over the drinks. "Did you have any children?"

"No. You?"

"A little boy."

"And a total cutie." Autumn bopped over, stuffing change into her pocket. "Owen is the sweetest little boy."

"I think so, but then I'm biased." Sierra's eyes misted. "You two have someone waiting for you. I can feel him glowering from here."

"That would be Justin." Autumn rolled her eyes, as if both a touch amused and exasperated by her older brother. "Let him wait. He needs to learn to be more patient. This will be a good opportunity for him."

"Or a good opportunity for him to lose his temper." Rori bit her lip, nodded goodbye to Sierra and took a sip of her milkshake. Nothing came up the straw.

"I'm not afraid of that man's temper." Autumn

plopped her Stetson onto her head and led the way out the door. Fearless, that was Autumn. She might look frail, but she knew how to hold her own. She marched right up to her brother, who leaned against the building, a harsh scowl somehow making him look more handsome.

Rori's pulse fluttered in admiration and in memory. She knew how tender Justin's voice could be when he leaned close to murmur in her ear. The memory of sitting on the porch swing rushed back to her, Justin's strong arm cradling her shoulder. The innocent thrill of being close to him whispered through her now, as sweet as the evening breeze.

The distance between them vanished when his gaze fastened on hers. Autumn stood between them, the rumble of a motorcycle rolled down the street, and Copper's whinny of greeting faded into nothingness. All that surrounded her, all that she could see, was Justin tall and strong in the golden evening light and his emotions revealed.

Was that regret she saw? A wish for what could have been? The concrete beneath her old riding boots faltered. She froze, unable to trust her next step. The moment stretched, timeless, and she felt the beat of his heart. Was he remembering, too? Was he wishing there was a chance? Her entire being leaned toward him and the past vanished. For one moment, it was as if there had been no breakup, no anger and hurt or disappointment. That no years separated them, and no distance. She felt his affection as unmistakable as the sun skimming her cheek.

Hope burst through her. "Justin, I—"

He closed up like night falling. His eyes shielded. His face hardened. He turned away, and she stood in darkness, cold where once she'd been warm, her hopes scattered like rattling October leaves on the ground in front of her.

"Autumn, I need to talk with you." Justin turned his back, hauling his sister with him by the arm.

Alone, Rori blinked against the sun in her eyes, the sun she could not feel. Humiliation washed over her. Had she been wrong? Had she only imagined what Justin felt, that he might be regretting his decision like she did and he was wondering if—

That was one *if* she could not let herself imagine. Not ever again. Marriage hadn't worked out so well for her, and she wasn't eager to do it again. She swallowed hard, willing down a pain she could not let him see. Copper nickered, stretching his nose as far as his tether would allow, reaching out to her as if he'd seen it all and had understood everything.

It was nice to have a champion and a true friend. She wrapped one arm around his neck. Burying her face in the velvet heat of his coat, she breathed in his comforting scent. He nickered low in his throat, as if offering sympathy.

"Thanks, buddy," she whispered so only he could hear. He tossed his head, craning to get a look at what she had a hold of. "Oh, right. I'd forgotten."

Where time went, she had no clue. But the years had changed so many things. This wasn't one of them. She popped the top from the cup, pulled out the straw and let him lap it up. Companionably, she licked the thick blob of milkshake that clung to the straw and the ache in her soul eased a little. By the time the horse had licked the inside of the cup dry, Autumn returned.

"Justin wants me to come home. Three out of the last

four mares are about ready to foal." Autumn returned and untied Bella, her movements uncharacteristically jerky. "My one evening off."

"A rancher's work is never done?"

"I know, but I have the right to complain, don't I?" She grinned.

"Justin said something else that upset you," she guessed because Autumn loved her work.

"True." Autumn mounted up. "I'm sorry for Justin. He was rude to you."

"He was sending me a message." Her face heated. Had he recognized her affection? Had he guessed at what she'd been feeling?

Probably. Humiliation washed through her. As if she didn't feel badly enough. "Guess I'll see you tomorrow."

"I'm going to talk to him. He shouldn't be treating you like that."

"No, but we'll work it out. Don't say anything. Please."

"Okay, as your friend. But if he keeps this up, I won't be able to ignore it."

The back of her neck prickled. She tossed the empty cup into the nearby garbage can and caught sight of Justin's pickup idling a good ten yards away, brake lights lit. Obviously, he was waiting for his sister. There was a steel wall between them. She felt nothing, not even his coldness toward her.

"I hate leaving you like this," Autumn explained. "Dad is calling everyone in. They need me to help."

"I wanted to take the scenic ride home anyway." She untied Copper's reins. "I'll be keeping you all in my prayers."

"Thanks." Autumn waved goodbye, wheeling her beautiful horse around in the street and taking off at a fast trot. The steeled horse clip-clopped on the pavement as she followed Justin's truck.

"Guess it's just you and me, buddy." She mounted up, the leather creaking as she settled into the saddle. Justin's truck grew smaller with distance until the sun's glare stole him from her sight.

She'd become lost in time today, her feelings tangled up with the past. She couldn't afford to get confused like that again. No more wishing for what might be, she told herself. Careful choices, that was her plan. There was no way Justin could ever be considered a good choice and certainly not Justin as he was today. Where did the gentle young man he'd been go?

That was the man she missed, she realized, gathering Copper's reins. A man who no longer existed. He was as lost to her as the young woman she'd once been, full of naivety and unrealistic expectations.

"C'mon, boy. Let's head home." Justin's rebuff still hurt, but she would have to get over it. He'd made his feelings plain.

Copper answered with a whinny and led the way, taking off down the street in a sprightly walk. Show horse that he'd once been, he held his head high and tossed his mane, earning admiration from a little girl and her mom climbing out of their four-wheel drive.

"Rori Cornell, is that you?" Eva Gibbs called out over the top of her Jeep. "Are you coming to Terri's wedding?"

"I am."

"Then I'm telling the old gang. I'll see you on Saturday."

"I can't wait." Yes, it was good to be home again. She'd missed the people and this way of life more than she'd realized. She dropped the reins over the saddle horn, giving Copper his head. As he broke into a cantor, she felt a little bit more like the girl she used to be.

"Go to bed, Dad." Justin grabbed the steaming carafe of fresh-brewed coffee. "I'll keep an eye on things tonight."

"No, that's not fair. We'll split the duty." Frank set a thermos on the counter, his face tight with strain. "I'll take first shift so you can get some shut-eye."

Justin snatched the thermos away from his father and filled it over the sink. "I'll be up anyway."

"Got trouble on your mind?"

"You could say that." No way was he letting his dad know what—or rather who—was troubling him. Dad probably already had it figured out. Besides, with one foal dropped and two more about ready, trouble was at the foremost of all of their minds. "Don't even mention Rori."

"Fine. I was going to say I think Sunny is about ready to go. I'll be staying out in the barn. If you stay with me, then Autumn can relieve you in the morning."

"So much for getting some shut-eye." Justin screwed the cup onto the top of the thermos and tucked it under his arm. The screen door slapped shut behind him as he padded down the steps.

The moon was full tonight, blazing the hillsides and meadows with luminous platinum and highlighting Autumn kneeling beside a mare in the corral.

"Is Paullina close, too?" He kept his voice low, but it carried easily in the midnight hush. That would be four out of four, an even busier night.

"No, she's resting. I spotted a pack of coyotes up against the tree line when I came out here. You will need to keep a close eye on her, though."

"I promise. I'll take good care of her."

"I appreciate it. Justin—"

He recognized the tone, and it meant she wanted to talk about something important. Ten to one that something important was Rori. "I don't want to talk about her."

"But—"

"No buts." He pushed away from the fence. "You can't fix everything, Autumn."

"Maybe if you tried to forget."

"Forget what? Her wanting something more than me?" He hid the pain as best he could behind a smile. "Take a look at me. Can you blame her? There was a reason she graduated top of her class. She's no dummy."

"No, but you can be one."

"No argument there." It mattered that his sister cared, but some things hurt too much. Like seeing Rori in town.

She'd come back and fit into life, looking right at home as if she had never left. As if time and their differences hadn't torn him apart. He could have almost believed that she was waiting for him, just as she'd done long ago, with a strawberry milkshake sitting on the table in front of her and Copper tied at the hitching post. Did she remember? Or had it all been easily forgotten?

As long as he kept himself as stone-hard on the inside, he wouldn't have to feel or hope or start wishing for what wasn't meant to be. Rori may be fitting in just fine, but she was still the same girl, ready to leave him behind.

Help me to remember that, Lord. He tipped his head and stared straight up at the heavens. Stars winked and the moon glowed against infinite black. Somewhere God was out there, watching over them all. He felt closer tonight.

Headlights broke the night darkness, hovering above the inky driveway. It took him a moment to place the truck.

"Cheyenne!" Autumn launched through the fence and pelted down the driveway. The truck halted a few yards short of the garage, and the driver's door flung open. His sister emerged, shouting with glee. Autumn launched at her and they hugged, jumping and squealing.

It was good Cheyenne was safely home.

"Is that you, girl?" The back door swung open, the porch light went on.

"Daddy!" Cheyenne shouted, extricating herself from Autumn's hug and racing across the yard. She jumped into her father's arms.

Dad's deep happy chuckle rumbled through the night. "Glad to see you, young lady."

"Cheyenne!" Addison stumbled out in her house-coat, hair tousled from sleep. "You're home! You've got to see the foal!"

Too much emotion for him, and besides, there was work to be done. Justin hiked toward the barn. He shut the doors behind him, cutting out all sounds of happiness and joy, of homecoming and family love that threatened to pull him back and remember dreams he'd lost along the way.

Alone, he ambled down the aisle, talking low and comforting to the mare awaiting his care.

Chapter Seven

❧

Weddings. He didn't like them. Justin had wanted to avoid this one, but his entire family had dragged him along. Since Rori was attending the reception, too, his torture continued.

Why couldn't he block her from his mind? He accepted a dainty glass cup full of lemonade from elderly Mrs. Ford, doing his best not to grumble at the too-small handle he couldn't get his fingers through. His dad was having the same problem, but nothing seemed to trouble Frank. He cradled the cup in one hand, hardly noticing it as he chatted with the mayor's wife.

Great. This was what he got for agreeing to share a ride with his father. It didn't look as if they would leave any time soon. Justin ran a finger behind his collar, hating the tie that cinched him up like a noose. Social events didn't usually put him on edge, but this one was destined to. He spotted Rori standing alone on the periphery of the crowd.

She made a pretty picture in the dappled sunshine wearing a sleek blue dress that exactly matched her eyes and her hair rippling in the breeze. He kept his resolve in place. He had to turn his back on her. They couldn't be friends; he couldn't take it. So that didn't leave him with any other choice.

"Cady ought to be here." Martha Wisener's voice rose above the din of the crowd and the classical music screeching over in the corner. He was not a fan of the violin. He tried not to listen, but the mayor's wife was a gregarious sort with a voice to match. "She closes on the lodge on Monday, so she's staying at a hotel over in Sunshine until then. She's moved all the way from New York, can you imagine? She's never been out west before her one trip here."

"You don't say?" Dad seemed interested in that. "She and her husband just decided to up and move?"

"Oh, there's no husband. Cady Winslow is a single lady. Always has been. Just a real classy gal and as nice as could be."

Doubtful, Justin thought, fighting a sadness he didn't want to admit. It was easier to stick with the notion that no woman was trustworthy, that you couldn't depend on a single one of them.

Take Rori. She stood like an outsider who didn't belong, watching the kids dashing around trees and squealing down the sidewalk, playing tag in front of the church. She looked lonely. He'd hurt her the other day. He didn't like it, but he couldn't apologize for it either. Seeing her threatened the careful defenses he'd set up against her. Tiny curls of emotion struggled to escape, and a tough man wouldn't give in to those tender feelings. Nothing good could come of it.

"I'm still mad at you." Autumn sidled up to him, a plate of wedding cake in one hand and a fork in the other. "You're being impossible."

"No, I'm being smart." He'd been successfully avoiding Rori for days. He didn't see why he should break his streak now.

"Smart? I don't think so. How about cowardly?"

"I'm not a coward." He ground out the words. Maybe he was so prickly because they just might be true. He wasn't handling the Rori situation well at all. "I don't want to talk about her."

"You're going to have to eventually. She works on the ranch. She lives in the same town. You can't keep changing directions and going the other way every time you two meet. It might as well be sooner rather than later."

"I disagree. I'm perfectly happy standing here ignoring her."

"But she isn't. Look at her. She's alone. Now's the perfect opportunity."

"Don't you have someone else to bother?"

"No one as fun as you." She smiled up at him, understanding what he couldn't say. "I didn't realize how you still felt about her."

"And trying not to." Trying for all he was worth. He wanted those feelings to be gone. He wanted them crushed to bits, tossed over the edge of a high cliff and scattered on the wind never to be seen again. But wanting didn't make it so. Even with his spine set and his feet planted with determination something deep within him whispered to turn around and look at her. Somehow he could feel her loneliness and her misery. Not that she would admit to being miserable, but he could feel it. He'd put that misery there.

"Don't you say a thing to her, do you hear me?" He knew he sounded like a bear, but the thought of opening up riled him. Better to act angry now than to wind up heartbroken later. "You keep this secret between the two of us."

"Well, maybe the three of us." Dad ambled over, frowned at the itty bitty cup he held and drained it in a single swallow. "Couldn't help overhearing, mostly because I was trying to."

"I knew coming here was a bad idea."

"We've all known Terri since she was knee-high. It's not like we want to miss being here for her." He set the cup on the edge of a nearby table. "Do you want to know how I know you're still hung up on Rori?"

"You're wrong, Dad."

"Because you're working so hard to ignore her. Son, if you're really over her like you say, then you would have no problem going over there and asking her to dance."

"Like I need your romantic advice? You haven't dated a woman in over thirty years."

"True, but I was a charmer in my day." That was how he caught the prettiest gal in White Horse County. "Go on over there and ask the poor girl. If you do it, I won't say another word about the two of you."

"Unbelievable. Besides, Rori's not standing alone anymore. I'm through with the both of you. I'm gonna go get some cake." He stalked away, shaking his head, looking as if he was trying to work up a storm of mad to keep painful things at bay.

"What are we going to do about him?" Autumn stabbed her fork into her piece of cake and scraped off the frosting.

"I don't know. I reckon he and Rori will figure it out. What are you doing, kid? The frosting is the best part."

"Sure, but it's really bad for you."

"That won't stop me." He scooped a chunk of white

fluff from the edge of the plate, using his finger since no one was looking.

"I wonder who that is?" Autumn asked, gesturing with her fork down the sidewalk.

"Who?" Instead of swiping another bit of frosting, he squinted into the bright rays of the sun.

A woman tapped their way, no one he'd seen before in these parts. She looked to be somewhere in her mid to late forties, tall and willowy, and she moved gracefully, as if the sun burnishing her slender shoulders shone just for her. Her light brown hair was shoulder length with a fancy cut and highlights—he had three daughters, so he wasn't unfamiliar with such things. She wore a simple slim green dress and matching heels. A few steps closer brought her face into view—heart-shaped, flawless skin and a radiance that could bring a man to his knees.

"Cady!" Martha, the mayor's wife, broke off from her crowd and hurried across the lawn. "You did make it."

"Barely. I'm so sorry I missed the ceremony." The woman named Cady smiled. She could have been a movie star with that wide, friendly smile, one that lit her up and everything around her. "I ran into road construction all through South Dakota, which made me a full day late. I just made it in."

"Then we're happy you're here safe and sound." Martha wrapped the woman in a warm hug.

"Must be the lodge's new owner," Autumn told him, as if he hadn't figured that out for himself. "I talked with her on the phone, so I recognize her voice. She's really nice."

He didn't need anyone's help to figure that out either. If he looked up "nice" in the dictionary, he wouldn't be surprised to see a picture of this Cady woman posted there. She looked like goodness walking, a dream men like him had forgotten to believe in.

The mayor hurried over, blocking his view, and Frank took it as a sign. No sense in watching the woman or in bothering to join the crowd greeting her. He was a practical sort with his feet firmly planted on the ground. He'd learned the hard way that dreams had a way of breaking a man. He'd been burned by a city woman before. He turned his back to her and headed for the dessert table, where he spotted his son working on a piece of cake. Cake. Now that was a good distraction.

"Maybe I'm wrong, but is Justin looking our way?" Eva Gibbs asked over the lilt of the string quartet playing on the church's side lawn. The hall's carpet hadn't dried out quick enough after all, so Terri's wedding reception had been moved outdoors.

Rori didn't dare look over her shoulder like the rest of her high-school friends. As if she wanted the man to think she might be talking about him! He'd made his feelings toward her crystal clear, and she intended to keep her distance and her dignity. The only thing left to do was to figure out a way to be immune to him.

"You're wrong, Eva. He's not looking at us, he's looking at *Rori,*" Marjorie Long announced with a wink. "You know what they say about first love?"

"I do, but I don't believe it," Rori quipped. Her biggest fear was that her friends were going to read something into this, and somehow she had to keep unaffected and aloof. If he really was watching, she didn't want him to know how hard this was for her. "Besides, Justin isn't my first love."

"Then who was?" Eva wanted to know.

"Copper." That brought a round of laughter from the little circle of her oldest friends. She couldn't help laughing, too. "Copper is a good guy. He's loyal and agreeable."

"Plus you can tell him what to do and he does it," Eva added. "I wish my husband was more like Copper."

"Hey, I heard that!" a man called out from a nearby cluster of guys, who all looked familiar. Rori recognized Eva's husband, Gary, who'd been senior class president.

"See what I have to put up with?" he asked his buddies, his good nature ringing in his voice. "If you fellas will excuse me, I need to set my wife straight on a few things. Eva, may I have this dance?"

"Certainly." Eva beamed, allowing her husband to take her hand and escort her over to the shade beneath several ancient maple trees. They joined in with the others waltzing in the dazzling afternoon.

"I'm going to get a refill." Sierra held up her empty cup. "Can I get anyone else one?"

"I'll come with you." Marjorie drained the last of her punch and the two of them headed off with promises to return.

Alone again and with no one to distract her, she could feel Justin's piercing stare from across the yard. She shivered as if in warning, although the breeze was hot, and she wasn't surprised when footfalls padded behind her in the grass. She set her jaw.

"Rori?"

Her name on his voice still rumbled deep like harmony, the sound she had once most loved to hear. She didn't turn, taking a moment to gather her courage.

"Aren't you going to speak to me?"

Did he sound glad or sorry for her silence? She

couldn't tell. Her fingers tightened on the glass handle of the cup she held and she turned toward him, dread rolling through her. Don't let him see it, she told herself. Don't let him know how much he hurt you.

"So, at least you're looking at me." No one was more handsome than Justin Granger in a suit and tie. He towered above her, dark hair tousled by the gentle breeze, as rugged as ever. "You're pretty ticked at me."

"No." She wasn't mad. Once, he would have been able to read her like a book but now he had no clue about her. She could see that plainly, too, and it was proof how much times had changed, how much *they* had changed. A touch of panic popped through her. All she could see was the image of him turning his back to her in front of the diner and of his empty chair at every meal she put on the Grangers' kitchen table. It wasn't as easy to hold back her feelings as she'd thought. How did he do it? She backed away. "Excuse me, but I have to go."

"Go where?" His hand snared her forearm, his fingers banding her wrist. His touch burned through her like a brand that would not yield and, worse, with recognition. One kindred soul recognizing another.

We are no longer like souls, she argued and wrenched away from his grip. But he held on, iron that would not relent.

"If you leave, then this awkwardness between us stays. And I don't want that." A muscle ticked in his jaw. At least she wasn't the only one tense; at least this was hard on him, too. He blew out a frustrated sigh. "Do you think it was easy for me to come over to you?"

"I don't understand what you think might solve this. We can agree to get along, but we tried that before, remember?"

"I remember. Friendly didn't work. That was my fault. I didn't realize how hard it would be." He told her the truth.

"It was hard to be friendly to me?"

Of course she had to take it the wrong way—and that was his fault, too. He counted to three and tried again. "Being friendly makes me remember the way things were."

"Me, too." She softened, her violet-blue eyes full of emotions that could tempt him to fall for her all over again. "Why is it that the bad times stick?"

"You mean like the time when you wouldn't accept my engagement ring?" How a decade-old wound could hurt as if it were new was a mystery he could not explain, but he felt the blow of it deep in his chest.

"You mean the way you didn't offer to wait for me?" The same wound was mirrored in her eyes, on her face, in her voice. "It was only four years until I graduated."

"You wanted me to wait?" That had never occurred to him. He hung his head, disbelieving. Hard to believe he'd been that stubborn and unable to see what she'd needed. There was proof right there he would have made her a lousy husband. Maybe that was his real fear deep down, the one that had made him run and kept him running.

"I don't know about you, but I've had enough of bad times."

Her chin went up, and she gave nothing away. Not a hint of just how angry she was at him or of any other emotion. She was stronger than he realized.

"Then we'll concentrate on the good ones." He tugged her closer. "Come dance with me."

"Did I hear you right? You couldn't have asked—"

"I did." He led her along, stumbling across the grass. "Look at everyone. My family. Half our friends."

"They're watching us." She went pale, and he felt her tremble with nerves.

So, she wasn't as unaffected as he'd thought. Her vulnerability touched him. He couldn't let his defenses weaken. No tenderness allowed. He straightened his spine, determined to do this right. "If we don't do this, then you know what happens?"

"We're the talk of the town."

"And my family will never let me live it down. They will never leave the subject of you and me alone. But if we have one waltz, and you go on to dance with someone else and I do the same, then it's over. No one is going to keep wondering." He no longer was. "I want to put an end to this. Do you?"

"Yes." They were in the shadow of the maples surrounded by other dancing couples, and she placed her free hand on his shoulder.

You feel nothing, he ordered as he took the first step, guiding her to the sway of the music. Be cold. Be distant.

"The last time we danced like this was at my grandparents' fortieth wedding anniversary." Her voice teased him, pulling him back to what might have been.

He gritted his teeth, his will unyielding. He would not remember.

If only he could forget. The sound of the big band, scratchy on the old record player, the scents of honeysuckle blooming in her grandparents' garden and of berry punch from the big bowl on the porch table carried on the wind. How Rori, sweeter than sugarplums, twirled in his arms in a slow waltz beneath a fiery sunset.

"That was one good time." She could lull him into remembering more, if he let her.

It had been quite a night. She'd looked like a princess

in a white dress, all that had been missing was a tiara and the storybook ending to go with it. Even a man as cautious as he had believed that's where they were heading, for her hand had been cradled softly in his and her head rested on his shoulder. Tenderness had swept him away more strongly than any fairy tale.

"Surely we can think of another." She gazed up at him more lovely for all the years that had passed. She captivated just as much as she'd had in their school days. Rori had an open honesty that reeled him in against his will.

"There was that time we rode the horses to the river." He had more common sense than to bring up that stellar afternoon, but he did it anyway. The buried memories unearthed, he felt the heat of the late summer afternoon, smelled the sun-ripened grass and cottonwoods and maples baking in the hot wind. Heard again the hushed gurgle of the swift current and the horses blowing out their pleasure at the sight of the sparkling water up ahead.

"We rode to the river a hundred times." Amused, little dimples bookended her grin and he wondered what had put the brightness into her at the memory. "You aren't going to remind me of the first time I tried going off the rope swing, are you?"

"Guilty." He kept their three-step slow and easy and enough space between them so everyone was clear, especially his family, that this was a dance for old times' sake. There was nothing between them. Back then, their first trip to the river had been their first time alone together without family or friends from school tagging along. "You were afraid to jump."

"I was," she agreed. "After you talked me into giving

it a try and I finally climbed onto that rope and put one foot on the big knot in the end, remember?"

"Sure do." As if he could ever forget the way she'd clung to that sturdy hemp, her hair tied back in a single ponytail, wearing a pink T-shirt and ragged cutoffs, the gold cross around her neck glinting in the sun. He'd been treading water, ready to help her to shore, and tried to talk her through it. He'd been chagrined to learn she was afraid of heights and between the tree, the rope and the steep cut of the bank, it was a fair way to the river.

"If I recall correctly," he drawled. "I said trust me, I won't let anything bad happen to you."

"And I closed my eyes and jumped. I trusted you."

"Bad decision," he quipped, surprised when a chuckle rumbled through him. She laughed, too, and the sounds merged like melody and harmony and in perfect synchrony. Just like old times.

"I remember Gram packed us a tasty picnic lunch and after you rode home with me, you kissed me." Her blue-as-dream eyes resonated with the innocence of that time and the beauty. "Not a peck on the cheek, as you had done before, but a real kiss. It was everything a girl's first kiss should be. Sweet and gentle and reverent."

"The Granger men are gentlemen, even if we spend most of the day with horses and cattle." Humor was the best way to hide the fact that he recalled that kiss, too, how she'd looked too lovely beneath the lilac tree in front of her grandparents' house. When their lips had met for the first time, he'd seen his future loving her, protecting her, taking care of her and making sure she spent the rest of her life happy.

But he never got the chance. They never got their ever

after. The music began winding down and couples around them broke apart, and a prayer rose straight from his soul. *Lord, please don't let this moment end.*

Chapter Eight

"You were always a perfect gentleman to me." Rori gave in and let her eyes drift shut. Justin led her in the final few steps of the dance. They were the only couple on the dance floor still together, as if trying to hold back the last notes of the music. "I never thanked you for that."

"No need." His voice was a few notes deeper than that of the boy from that long-ago night, his shoulders wider, a hint of a five-o'clock shadow on his jaw, but his strength of principles remained. The dance was over, the last note faded into the brilliant May afternoon.

She opened her eyes, the moment broken, the past vanished. All that stood between them were the remnants of a shared past that could no longer be. Their chance was gone, but she couldn't stop the piece of her soul that wished and whispered. What would have happened if she'd accepted his proposal?

When she opened her eyes, she realized he hadn't moved away. Couples surrounding them were chatting and the kids' shrieks of delight carried above the roar and rumble of conversations. The sunshine, suddenly too bright, made her eyes burn.

"Are you okay?" Justin asked, towering above her, his baritone buttery warm with concern.

If he'd been cold or distant or dismissive, she could have handled it better than his caring. How had she gotten carried away? A dignified woman gathered her feelings, hid them carefully for none to see and pasted a polite smile on her face. "Thank you for the dance."

"It was my pleasure." He turned away as if it were the easiest thing in the world and offered her a small smile, neither cold nor caring but one of recognition of what they'd once been. Beyond the bitterness, beyond all hope.

"We had better stick to the plan," he said over his shoulder, tossing a glance toward the punch table.

His family must be there, she surmised, because she wasn't about to look. She tried to make her feet work so she wouldn't seem like a fool staring after him, as if she still carried a torch, but she didn't move fast enough. Justin had asked Eva to dance, stealing her away from Gary as the first notes of the next waltz filled the air like a new beginning.

Alone, Rori hurried out from beneath the maples, wondering just who had noticed.

"You're lookin' mighty lonely, young lady." Frank Granger called her back. "You wouldn't want to give an old cowboy like me the pleasure of this dance?"

"I would be honored. Under one condition." Out of the corner of her eye, she saw Justin guiding Eva step by step, talking easily. She'd let go of the past. Now it was time to move on. She was grateful to Justin's dad for his offer. She knew what he was doing, helping to ease her embarrassment and keeping her from deciding to head home. "We don't mention Justin."

"Deal." Frank offered his hand. "I figure I'll be lucky to get a few turns around the dance floor before the young bucks in this town start taking a shine to you. Look, there's one now."

It turned out Frank was right. Less than a minute into their dance, Troy Walters cut in. She did her best not to notice Justin, who had relinquished Eva to her husband's arms before he wandered off. She had to close her heart against him. It was better for both of them that way.

His dad did that on purpose. Justin grabbed a handful of cashews from the bowl on the table and popped a few into his mouth. Asking Rori to dance and then handing her over to Troy. The cowpoke was still dancing with her and judging by the look of things, she enjoyed being with him.

Shouldn't he be glad? His plan was working. His dad and sisters had said nothing about him and Rori. He took a swig of punch to wash down the nuts and they caught in his throat. Truth be told, he wasn't glad at all. Rori looked right at home in Troy's arms, and the crimson staining the edges of his vision was jealousy, plain and simple.

The current dance ended, and Justin watched as his dad escorted his dance partner back to the circle of folding chairs set out in the church's shade. Elderly Mrs. Tipple beamed with delight as she joined her friends. Another elderly widow spoke hopefully to Dad, and he nodded, offering his arm to her.

"Saw you and Rori dancing." Blake Parnell moseyed up to the table and grabbed a handful of cashews. "Guess old high-school sweethearts can still be friends."

"Guess so." He couldn't stop from noticing that Rori had stopped dancing and accompanied Troy off the dance area to a group of friends. Since he didn't want to get caught staring after his old sweetheart, he focused in on Blake. "The Marines let you off for good behavior?"

"Me? I'm never good." Blake's severe military haircut and drilled-in soldier stance belied his statement. He was special forces, the elite of the elite. He was Terri's cousin. "I flew in last night. Almost didn't make it for Terri's big day. With her dad gone, I'm not sure what she would have done to me if I hadn't been able to walk her down the aisle."

"She and Tom make a good pair." Small talk kept his mind busy. Maybe there was a chance he could forget about Rori entirely. "How long are you home for?"

"The weekend. I head back on Monday."

"Didn't you just get back from Afghanistan?" Something blue at the corner of his field of vision caught his attention. Rori. He gritted his teeth, refusing to look.

"Yep. I'm about ready to leave for a year in Okinawa. Looks like Terri's almost ready to go. They're bringing around the car. See you later, Justin."

"See ya." Sure enough, a brown sedan decorated with ribbons and bows glided to a stop in front of the church. Shouts rose up, folks cheering as they headed over to line the concrete pathway.

Time to go, he decided. His obligation here was done, and just in time because his sisters had clustered around Rori, pulling her toward the front step.

He could still feel her in his arms.

"Single ladies! Up front!" the mayor's wife hollered above the din. "Time for the bouquet."

The bride pounded onto the top step, her elaborate

white gown swaying. As if he needed to see this, he thought, hiking off toward the quiet side of the church. He didn't need to think about Rori single again and how she'd laughed in her gentle way when Troy had whirled her waltz after waltz.

"Hold up, son." Frank jogged after him. "I'll come with you."

"I don't want to leave the ranch unattended for long." The only concern was Paullina, their last expecting mare, although she wasn't the most important reason why he wanted to leave.

A roar rose up above laughter and hoots and hollers as the bride feigned a throw. A few of the town's more aggressive single ladies leaped into the air like NFL quarterbacks at the Super Bowl. Rori wasn't one of them.

At the sight of her, the memory of her in his arms returned.

"Guess I was right," Frank said in that affable way of his. "All you and Rori needed to do was to clear the air. You look more like your old self."

Maybe his father thought so, but Justin didn't agree. It was hard work to hide his scowl. The rising tide of jealousy just kept coming at him and he couldn't shake the feeling he was leaving something important behind, something he might never find again.

"Isn't that Mrs. Tipple's car?" Frank knelt down beside the 1963 Falcon, which was still in showroom condition. "She's got a flat."

"I'll check her spare." Justin opened the driver's door and pulled down the sun visor. He caught the set of keys that fell from it and unlocked the trunk. "She has a jack and a tire iron in here, but the spare is flat."

"Then I'll roll it down to the gas station."

"No, I'll do it." He didn't mind helping out. He would rather be busy, that way he didn't have to think about Rori and Troy, or Rori and any other bachelor in these parts.

All he wanted to do was to forget her.

"Okay, this time is for real!" Terri called over her shoulder, clutching the bouquet in both hands. She bent her knees deep, as if ready to hurl it into space. "One, two, three—"

The beribboned spray arced into the air, thudded against the underside of the entrance's awning and ricocheted straight toward the flowerbeds. Rori, having chosen the outer perimeter of the crowd hoping to avoid the bouquet, looked up just in time. Bachelorettes were leaping, others shouted and arms reached out and fell short as the flowers jettisoned straight at her head.

Duck. That was her first instinct. She did *not* want to catch those flowers. But who knew what unsuspecting elderly widow was standing behind her innocently chatting with her friends? So, to avoid any accidental injuries, she reached out and caught the bunch of perfect roses.

"Rori! You did it!" Autumn shrieked, clapping enthusiastically. "Congratulations."

"Looks like you're going to be next." Cheyenne tossed a lock of dark auburn hair behind her shoulder before she gave Rori a hug. "And before you say that your divorce isn't final yet, you don't know what God has in store for you. Maybe happiness is waiting just around the corner."

"That's awfully optimistic." Rori shrugged. "The flowers hit the awning, that's why it came to me. The bouquet was probably destined for one of you. Addison was standing directly behind Terri."

"Hey, I was dragged there. I don't want to get married." The youngest Granger sister spoke up, scrunching her button face in an amusing sneer. "Are you kidding? I don't want to give up my freedom. I don't want some man telling me what to do."

"She watches too many daytime talk shows," Autumn joked as they all moved together to the side of the pathway.

"Congratulations, dear." A frail voice, hardly audible in the din, made Rori turn. Mrs. Tipple was one of her grandmother's dearest friends. "I saw you were the belle of the ball, dancing with a few handsome men. I'm sure one of them will sweep you off your feet."

She'd been swept off her feet and she didn't know how to tell the dear lady that falling in love was the last thing she wanted to do again. From now on her motto was both feet on the ground and no one—not even Justin—was going to get control over her heart. She'd lost her illusions of love. Shattered, they could never be made whole again.

"I'll be praying for you." Mrs. Tipple patted Rori's hand consolingly before she turned away to join her circle of friends.

Terri and Tom, arm in arm, alight with profound joy, paraded down the walkway to their waiting sedan.

"Have fun, you two!" someone called out to the happily married couple. Flower petals sailed up into the air, twisting and dancing to the ground like colorful snowflakes.

Cheers rose up, and Rori tucked the bouquet into the

crook of her arm so she could clap. She prayed for every happiness for them. She truly hoped their love would never waver and their ideals never fall.

"She is a beautiful bride," Autumn breathed as Tom held the door for his new wife and helped her onto the passenger seat. "When I get married, I want it to be just like this, at the church where Mom and Dad were married."

"And we were baptized," Cheyenne added. "I haven't given a thought to my wedding day. I need to get through my last year of vet school first. It's the toughest, and it's looming ahead of me. Maybe after I've graduated, I'll think about marrying the right guy."

"Are there really any Mr. Rights these days?" Rori brushed a fingertip over one fragile rosebud. Breathing in the fragrance, she remembered her wedding day. Her bouquet had been made of roses, too.

"Is being here hard for you?" Autumn asked as the newlyweds motored away.

"Not much." Fine, it wasn't the entire truth, but she wanted it to be. She wanted to be over the pain and the humiliation of having a man fall out of love with you—two men, actually. "Water under the bridge. Are you going to get married here, Cheyenne?"

"It depends on whether or not I get proposed to."

Was that a twinkle? Rori wasn't the only one who saw it. The remaining two Granger girls instantly began talking.

"What do you mean? Is it getting serious with Edward?" Autumn asked.

"Are you totally in love with him and you haven't even told us?" Addison demanded. "Now's the time. Inquiring minds want to know."

"Inquiring minds will just have to wait." Cheyenne

shook her head, scattering her long red curls over her shoulders. "School comes first for both of us. But I don't think either scenario is out of the realm of possibility."

"I knew it!" Autumn held up a fist, and Cheyenne bumped it with one of hers.

"We're taking it slow, so there's no need to get so excited. Honestly." Cheyenne did look pleased. "Rori, how about you?"

"What about me?"

"You're going to marry again, right? Or would you want a home wedding this time around?"

"I'm not planning on getting married again." She hoped not one of the sisters would notice her gaze straying to the disbursing crowd. Or the fact that she felt disappointed there was no sign of Justin. "Two failed relationships are enough for me."

"Won't you get lonely?" Cheyenne wanted to know.

"Cheyenne!" Addison planted her hands on her hips. "I can't believe you. A woman doesn't need a man to be happy. In fact, show me one woman who is happier with a man than without. That's what I want to see."

"Well, there's my grandmother." Rori couldn't help pointing out the truth. "I've watched my grandparents most of my life, and they are truly happy."

"Fine, there's one stellar exception," Addison relented. "But I'm talking about generalities here."

"All I want is a man who doesn't turn tail on me when I outride him," Autumn added. "I haven't had a date since I was nineteen. That's ten years. I'm about to give up hope completely."

"I guess we'll both wind up as old single ladies." Rori bent down and held out the bouquet. Eva's little girl had been staring at it wistfully and came forward, eyes hopeful. "At least I'll be in good company."

"I feel better all ready." Autumn smiled, and it was like the sun shining. It was hard to believe she would never find true love.

Then again, true love was a scarce commodity in this world.

"For me?" the little girl asked, hands reaching for the roses. "Really?"

"Every little bride needs a bouquet." Rori knelt down, relinquishing the perfect blossoms.

"Thank you!" With a flip of her blond hair, the girl darted away.

"That was nice." Cheyenne took Rori by the arm. "I guess big-city life hasn't changed you any."

"I guess not that much." She let Autumn take her other arm and they headed into the church to help with the cleanup. There were so many things she'd forgotten over the years—the ladies' aid, simple weddings and country girl friendships—the kind of friendships that nothing, not even time, could diminish.

"Rori, no one expected you to stay and help clean up." Martha Wisener strutted up to Rori in the hall's wide entrance. Being the mayor's wife had become such a habit that she naturally took charge whether she was actually appointed or not. "It was good of you."

"Just helping out like old times." Pitching in had felt like the right thing to do. Her grandparents had left long ago, and Autumn had promised to drive her home. Rori grabbed her purse and her sweater from the stack on the nearby tabletop.

A tall, slim woman wearing a designer dress and

three-hundred-dollar heels joined her at the table. Rori recognized the shoes since she'd had a similar pair. The woman didn't look familiar and she certainly didn't seem to be from around here, not with that upscale salon cut and color. She had to be somewhere in her forties, but her skin was flawless and smooth. Her blue eyes sparkled in a friendly way.

"I can't seem to find my purse. I wasn't sure about just leaving it like this, but everyone else seemed to be doing it." Her quiet alto resonated with kindness and a sense of discovery. "I also hear most people do not lock their doors here."

"And some even leave their car keys in the ignition." A habit she'd been trying to break Gramps of, but he was stubborn. She spotted a designer bag, probably worth much more than the shoes, and grabbed it by the butter-soft leather handle. "Wild Horse is a pretty safe place. Is this yours?"

"Yes, thank you." The woman smiled and took the bag.

"Cady!" Martha boomed. "I can't believe you stayed and helped, too. You don't officially live in this town yet."

"It will be official tomorrow."

Oh, the new lodge owner. Rori had heard about her from Autumn and the grapevine. Even her grandparents had talked about it. Back in the day, they had honeymooned at the once luxurious inn. She hooked her purse strap over her shoulder and turned, ready to join Autumn outside. But something outside the back window froze her in place.

Justin. He knelt with his father beside an old Falcon, tapping a hubcap into place. Frail Mrs. Tipple stood nearby, her hand on her heart, crooning her thanks.

"I don't know what I would have done if you boys

hadn't changed my tire for me." Her voice thinned, betraying her emotion. "The tow truck would charge me more than a week's groceries to have it changed."

"You'll still need to replace the one tire so you will have a functional spare," Justin explained, rising, his work done. "That ought to do for you now, ma'am."

"Frank Granger, you've raised a fine son." Mrs. Tipple nodded her approval. "And you aren't so bad yourself."

"I thank you for that, ma'am." Frank, tire iron in hand, rose to his six-foot-plus height. "You have any trouble, you can always give me a call."

"Isn't that nice of that man," Cady Winslow said, joining her at the window. "He isn't a relative of hers, is he?"

"No, he's just helping out. Frank's like that." It was Justin she couldn't take her eyes off, taking the tire iron from his dad and stowing it in the trunk.

You don't want him, she told herself. You don't want to care for any man.

"Oh, that's Frank Granger and his son." Martha squeezed in close to assess the situation. "They live out of town a ways."

"Granger? That's the name you gave me for the horses." The lady lit up. "I have an appointment on Monday with Autumn to look at a mare."

Outside the window, Justin shut the trunk, gave it a pat and lifted his hand in farewell to Mrs. Tipple. Rori's pulse lurched. What if he sensed her spying on him from the window? Thankfully he didn't look her way as he strode out of sight.

"You and I spoke on the phone the other day." Her brain kicked into gear and the conversation around her began to make sense. Now she could place the well-modulated voice, remembering her first day at the Grangers'. "I cook and keep house for the family."

"Oh, you answered the phone. I remember." She smiled. "You were so helpful."

"Just doing my job." She opened the door. "You are going to love Autumn's horses."

"That's good news."

"They are the most gorgeous creatures, with the sweetest disposition. I don't think you'll be disappointed."

"I appreciate knowing that. When it comes to horses, I'm completely out of my element. I've wanted my own mare since I was a little girl. I'm already so excited, I could burst." Had she said too much? She may as well have a neon sign around her neck shouting "city girl." But no one faulted her for being indecorously enthusiastic. The door swished shut and Cady returned to the window.

Her gaze didn't waver from the view of the robust, steady-looking man with a touch of gray at his temples. The elderly lady offered him a handful of dollar bills. Frank refused with clear denial and kindness softening his ruggedly handsome face. The way he stood with his boots planted and the well-cut suit framing his wide shoulders made him look like a Western legend who had just walked off the silver screen.

"Cady, are you all right? You look lost in thought," Martha spoke, startling her.

"I'm perfectly fine." Heat stained her face. She jerked away, hoping her feelings weren't transparent.

"You must be hungry. Why don't you join Tim and me for supper?" Martha held out her hand, the big diamonds and rubies of her many rings glittering. "The maid promised to have a roast waiting. There will be plenty."

"Thank you, but I need to get settled at the motel."

Funny how she couldn't seem to tear her gaze away from the man, who opened the door for the frailest elderly lady Cady had ever seen. After the woman had folded her tiny frame into the front seat, Frank Granger closed the door cordially.

My, wasn't he something?

Not that men were interested in a woman her age. She'd celebrated her fiftieth birthday three weeks ago. Cady sighed, staring down at her hands that not even the most expensive lotions could keep young. She forced herself to turn away from the window, when all she wanted was to look at him one more time.

Chapter Nine

"So, did you and Justin clear the air?" Autumn asked behind the wheel as she guided her pickup along the ribbon of country highway. Town had disappeared from the rearview and Jeremy Miller's fields stretched far and wide on one side of the road, the Parnells' in the other. Still irrigation wheels adorned the growing sugar beets, hay and wheat and at the top of a rise a green and yellow tractor churned up dust.

Rori took her time answering. "Do we have to talk about your brother?"

"Believe me, there are days I feel the same way about him."

"And what way would that be?"

"Like he's the most irritating, hardheaded man alive." Autumn shook her head, her red-gold hair dancing in the breeze from the window. She might be trying to look annoyed, but it was only a front. Beneath the annoyance was a sister's love for her brother. "Justin is just like Dad. You have no idea what it's like to work with the pair of them. It drives me nuts some days. They refuse to listen. They always think they are right. Dad has gotten better, but Justin just keeps getting more impossible."

"The years have changed him."

"It hasn't been for the better." Autumn said nothing more, although a frown creased her forehead.

Rori wanted to ask what that meant, but she bit her lip. Maybe it was wrong to be curious about Justin. She wanted to know more, but why? And what good could come of it? Their waltz was supposed to be a sign of moving on, and that's what she wanted to do. So why wasn't her heart listening?

The truck's windows were down, and she let the grass-scented air breeze over her face. It felt good, bringing up memories of riding to town with Gramps in his old truck, the radio crackling and spitting static, the radio that had always been persnickety. Before that, she remembered riding shotgun with Mom behind the wheel of their old Ford, her little sister standing on the hump on the floor behind the front bench seat, talking excitedly about what kind of ice cream she wanted at the drive-in.

How could she have forgotten how much she loved this place? When she'd left for college, a piece of her had always stayed behind here. She'd always intended to come back, but the Lord had seemed to lead her in another direction. And truthfully, there was another reason she'd stayed away. The thought of running into Justin in town, seeing him at church as a matter of course had been too painful. Her love for him, as young as she'd been, was true.

"He took it pretty hard when you wouldn't say yes." Autumn broke the silence. "I don't blame you. You were right. You were just out of school, and I think that's too young to marry for most folks. Look at my dad. He married Mom right out of high school and no matter how hard he tried, how hard they both tried, they couldn't make it work."

"But I hurt him."

"It's true. Justin was never the same after you left."

"Neither was I." Justin had been so hurt and angry, her quiet refusal had surprised him as much as it had her. So she'd earned her degree, applied for jobs and the teaching position at a reputable arts school had seemed heaven sent. She'd met her future husband and settled for a second-best life with Brad. Knowing the outcome made her feel as if she'd made the worse decisions.

Is there a way to find peace, Lord? The need for it rose like a storm within her, so powerful her throat closed up. Turmoil became a physical pain, needles twisting behind her ribs.

"About four years ago," Autumn said as she slowed the truck. A cow was standing on the road up ahead. "Justin starting seeing this gal from the next town over. Tia seemed nice enough. I never did feel comfortable with her, but she made Justin happy. He started whistling again when he worked, and he stopped being bitter. He was almost a pleasure to be around, the way he used to be."

Rori's stomach coiled tight. She knew there couldn't be a happy end to the story. The truck rolled to a stop and she opened her door. Hot air puffed over her as she dropped to the pavement. "What happened?"

"He never said. He simply ended it." Autumn climbed down and circled around the front of the truck. The cow, intent on trying to dislodge the reflective yellow marker in the middle of the road, looked up and casually flicked her tail. Autumn shook her head as if in disbelief. "Buttercup, is that you?"

The cow mooed as if to say, "Yep, it's me," and went back to work on the marker.

"How did she get out?" Autumn plodded up to the cow. "She's spoiled rotten. We can't herd her home. You wouldn't happen to have any candy on you?"

"Maybe some mints in my purse."

"Let's look. I don't have any molasses treats in my truck. Justin got stingy at the feed store last week." Autumn circled back to the truck, and so did Rori.

The cow watched them go and blinked her long curly lashes, waiting to see if something more interesting than the bright yellow square was going to appear.

Rori dug into her purse, hauled out her wallet and her cell and a stick of lip gloss. A roll of butterscotch candies sat in the very bottom along with a bit of spare change. She handed the candy to Autumn.

The cow's head came up as she scented the air. She bolted into action the moment Autumn tore open the roll. With an excited moo, she clattered across the pavement, grabbed a butterscotch with her long tongue and crunched on it happily.

The hum of an engine broke the serenity of the valley. Rori glanced behind her and, sure enough, there was a second truck approaching—a white truck.

Justin. Nerves prickled through her as if she'd fallen into a nettles patch. Sweat broke out on her palms and a longing to see the steady strength of him surprised her, the wish for him rising up unbidden and so powerful she could not stop it.

"Is that you, Buttercup?" The passenger door swung open and Frank hopped down. The fact that he wore a suit and tie didn't stop him from holding out his hands to the heifer. "What do you think you're doing, girl?"

Buttercup's chocolate-brown eyes melted as she spotted her favorite person. She streaked past Autumn and burrowed her rather substantial-size head into Frank's chest. He patted the cow's neck, talking low to her.

"Do you want me to walk her home?" Autumn offered, but her words came as if from a far distance.

Although Justin remained in the truck, disguised by the sun-glazed windshield, Rori could feel his gaze and his distance. She had to remind herself that she was moving on, but did her heart listen?

Not a chance. How did she force it to? She had no idea. Autumn's story about him rang in her mind, playing over and over like a song. He'd had his heart broken twice. Was that the reason he'd become so hard?

Sympathy for him filled her, and she didn't notice that Autumn was talking to her until the truck door shut. She blinked, realizing that Frank was on his cell, Autumn was behind the steering wheel and she was standing in the middle of the eastbound lane.

"Dad will take Buttercup in. She'll follow him like a puppy. The rest of us wouldn't have an easy time budging her." Autumn waited while Rori climbed in and buckled up before she hit the gas. The road carried them around a corner and to her grandparents' driveway.

From out in the field, Copper spotted them. His head swung up from the grass, his tail arched, he whinnied and took off at a full gallop for the corner post.

"I see he's still racing trucks." Autumn smiled as she pulled into the driveway and eased off the gas. "It's good to see he's still got the spirit at his age."

"Yes. Some things don't change. At least not yet." She

prayed Copper had a lot of good years left. He surely looked as if he did. He sped along the fence line, ears back, stretched out in a dead gallop, his joy as tangible as the hot puff of breeze on her face. It lifted her up to see her beautiful boy stretched out like a Thoroughbred at the homestretch. Autumn was kind enough to ease off the gas the last few yards of the driveway so that Copper sailed ahead, the clear winner. He knew it, celebrating with a rear kick and a flick of his mane.

"Good boy!" Rori congratulated when she climbed down from the truck, her heels a little wobbly in the loose gravel as she approached the fence. "You did it. You are my good winner."

Breathing hard, Copper preened before leaning over the fence for a well-deserved hug. Autumn wobbled over on her heels to pet the champion.

"Did you girls get everything squared away at the church?" Gramps called out, hauling a ladder as he came into sight.

"We sure tried to," Rori answered. "Gram has you changing the bird feeders."

"She surely does. Those hummingbirds get better treatment than I do." He winked. "Howdy, Autumn. Good to see you here again. I'm sure Polly has some lemonade and sugar cookies in the kitchen if you girls are interested."

"Maybe when we were ten," Rori teased.

"Right, I forget you two are all grown up. My apologies." Gramps shook his head. "I guess you'll always be those little girls riding in the fields to me. I forget how much time has gone by."

"Del? So *that's* where you've got off to," another voice called out cheerfully. Gram appeared around the apple tree, hands on her hips. "The hummingbirds are bombing me. They aren't happy their feeder isn't changed yet."

"I just took a moment to chat with the girls." Gramps shook his head as if he were perturbed, but in truth there was no mistaking the affection lighting him up. "Look at Autumn. Was she always that tall?"

"Goodness, she was at the wedding today. She's at church every Sunday." Gram shook her head good-naturedly. "Men. Don't see what's right in front of their noses. Oh! Did you see that?"

"I sure did. Kamikaze hummingbird. He nearly got you." Gramps chuckled. "It's a laugh a minute around this crazy farm. If you girls will excuse me, I'd best go change the feeder before those birds circle around for their next air strike."

"I should say so!" Gram's face wreathed with mirth. "Say, wasn't that a lovely wedding? Brings back memories. We had pink and white roses, too. Remember, honey?"

"Like it was yesterday," Gramps called over his shoulder as he trudged up to the house, Gram hurrying to join him.

"Well, I'd better go help Dad. If Buttercup is out, others could be, too." Autumn pushed away from the fence, her forehead furrowed. "Maybe we've got more problems than we think."

"I hope not." She knew this part of the county hadn't seen major rustling problems in a long time, but all things changed. "I'll see you in church tomorrow?"

"Count on it, although I might not be bright-eyed and bushy-tailed. We'll see." She climbed up into her truck. "Have a good evening, Rori."

"You, too." She waved her friend off, glad of Copper's company as the dust cloud faded. There was nothing like a little quiet time between a girl and her horse. "How about I go inside and change, grab something to read and come outside and hang with you?"

Copper tossed his head, as if to offer his horsy approval. She crunched through the loose gravel toward the house, where Gramps had placed and climbed the ladder. Gram waited nearby, offering helpful advice.

"You're tipping it, Del."

"What's a bit of spilled sugar water?" Gramps didn't seem troubled.

"It's wasteful, that's what, and I don't want ants congregating on my porch." Gram's eyes twinkled as she gazed up at her husband. "Over fifty years and I have to tell you every time."

"That's why I keep you around, Polly. To tell me things I don't have to bother to remember," Gramps quipped.

"Oh, you!" Gram laughed. "Rori! Did you girls have a fun time?"

"Very. Even the cleanup was fun. I got to catch up with old friends while I dried dishes."

"I was talking about all that dancing," Gram warbled, looking pleased.

Time to blush. Rori rolled her eyes. She should have guessed it would have been impossible to get through the evening without discussing Justin at least once.

"My, but you're popular." Gramps began his descent of the ladder. "No surprise there. You always were."

"I danced with two guys, that's it." And one only because it would prove to Justin she wasn't falling for him again.

"One is all it takes." Gram beamed. "There's plenty

of fine young men in this county. You'll be happily married in no time."

"You did catch that bouquet," Gramps pointed out, carefully transferring his weight from the bottom rung of the ladder to the ground. "I saw the way Justin Granger was looking at you. That boy's still sweet on you. Woo-wee."

Her defenses went up, but one look at the wishes sparkling on her grandparents' faces stopped her. How could she fault these people who had always championed her and who radiated their hopes for her happiness?

"No comment." She pleaded the fifth, since it had to be safer than trying to convince these two she wasn't falling in love with him again. It took everything she had to try to convince herself.

"Looks like we've got a problem," Justin said into his cell, staring at the cut wire and downed posts at the Granger/Cornell property line.

"You're not telling me something I don't already know." On the other end of the call, Frank was at a computer, and Justin could hear the rapid *tap, tap, tap* of the keys.

"Did the girls find any more cattle out?"

"Not that we can tell. I sent every hired man we had checking roads, driveways, you name it. Nothing."

"But we're still missing three cows?"

"So far. I got a call in to the sheriff, for all the good that will do. Autumn and the hired men are doing head counts and I'm going through records to make sure no other cows are missing."

"Maybe they just took the ones with access to the road."

"That's what I'm afraid of." The two-year-olds had

been bottle-fed and hand-raised, orphans who'd lost their mamas and were so tame anyone could walk up to them. Tame enough and well pedigreed so that they would fetch a high price at any auction in the state. "What did you find, son?"

"I know where they got in. Looks like a pair of motorcycle tracks. There's a lot of foliage here, a lot of cover from the road. No one would have noticed anything."

"Sure, since most everyone in these parts was at Terri and Tom's wedding."

Justin knew what his dad was thinking. Whoever had stolen from them had to know about the wedding, which would include half the county. Instead of an organized strike, this looked like a couple of people who probably hadn't been armed. He remembered the last time rustlers had troubled them. His dad had spent six weeks in intensive care. "At least they waited until everyone was gone."

"Thank God for small favors."

"I'll follow these tracks and see where they lead. You'll tell the sheriff?"

"Sure, when and if he shows up. Be careful, Justin. Whoever did this is probably long gone, but it doesn't hurt to play it safe."

"I know." He flipped shut his phone and swung up into his saddle. Max gave a mane toss, as if to say he was annoyed at this slow pace of things. Justin guided him through the downed length of the fence, careful not to disturb evidence should the sheriff want to take a look at it.

From his vantage in the saddle, he caught glimpses of the Cornell place through breaks in the trees. He spotted Copper grazing in his pasture, cropping the grass close to the house. His red coat shone in the sun and for some reason a memory burst into his mind, of Copper grazing next to Scout, both horses without saddles, their bridles trailing in the grasses. Again he heard the mighty sound of water splashing as Rori disappeared into the shining river, and droplets whooshed upward like pieces of crystal. He caught the rope, the hemp coarse in his hand, as he waited for her to surface.

She popped up, hair sleek and dark gold, her eyelashes damp and curling, delight turning her eyes a clear lavender. Her laughter trilled, his most favorite sound, as she treaded water and spotted him on the bank. "Your turn."

"You'd better watch out. I feel the need to cannonball." That was his only warning as he pulled the rope back, jumped up and held on tight. The world spun away beneath him, exhilarating and free. He sailed from the bank and high above the water, the hot June wind puffing against his face. He let go at the highest arc of the rope, spotting Rori in the river below, and curled up into a ball. Gravity pulled him down into the cool, refreshing wetness. He dropped down into the sun-streaked waters, where a trout scurried out of his way and Rori's pretty little feet were treading water.

Was it his fault his hand snaked out and grabbed her ankle? He gave a tug, drawing her down with him. He heard her shout of surprise, muffled by the water, and waited a beat so she could get a mouthful of air before he dragged her down with him. Her arms came around his shoulders, her hair loose and flowing like a mermaid's—his mermaid. The tender love that scored his soul was immeasurable. He swung her in a fast circle, the water whirling around them before he kicked up, lifting them to the surface. She came up laughing, her joy alive in his heart. She was his heart.

"I can't believe I'm graduating tonight." She took one hand off his shoulder to swipe at the water streaming into her eyes. Her church youth choir T-shirt glowed red as the sunlight found her. A dragonfly hovered close to check out the color before buzzing away.

"You're graduating in less than three hours." He checked his watch, which was waterproof, of course. "Your grandmother is going to kick me across a month of Sundays if I don't get you home soon."

"My gram has never kicked anyone in her life."

"That's what I mean. She'll bring out the special punishment for me. Tonight's important to her." He folded a lock of hair behind her ear. Her hair was like satin, her skin like silk. "One more jump and then I'm taking you home."

"Why? What's special about tonight?" She squinted at him, searching for the tiniest hint. "Don't tell me she has a party planned. I told her I didn't want a big fuss."

"I'm not saying a word. You can't get anything out of me." Laughter rumbled through him. He'd never been happier. The pieces of his life were coming together. He could finally see God's purpose for him—working the land as five generations of Grangers had before him, marrying Rori and taking care of her. Keeping her safe and happy and protected. Doing his utmost to give her a joyful life with all the love he possessed.

"Not a party." She rolled her eyes. "I suppose no one could stop her."

"Your grandmother is a determined woman." That was a fact. "You can be, too, Rori Cornell."

"True, but that's not all in all a bad thing. At least I'm not stubborn like you. Set in my ways." Gentle teasing. The love for him in her eyes was priceless. She had no idea how much it meant to him. How much he would give up for her, do for her.

"I'm not stubborn," he denied, although maybe it was true. Everyone said it was, but he couldn't see it. "I just know what I want."

And he wanted her. He wanted to spend every day, every season, every year with her for the rest of his life.

"Justin?" she asked, arms still looped around his neck. The laughter faded from her beautiful face, seriousness dulcet in her voice. "Tell me that nothing is going to change."

"Darlin', everything changes. But change can be for the good." Like weddings and starting a family and living happily ever after.

"Tell me that we aren't going to change. That no matter what, it will always be you and me."

The gurgling melody of the river, the blissful sunshine and the peace of that long-ago afternoon faded. Justin blinked, realizing something had pulled him from his daydream. He was surprised to find that he'd drawn Max to a stop and was staring at a perfect view of the Cornells' backyard. Del and Polly were side by side on a porch swing, Del reading a farming magazine, Polly her Bible.

Was Rori nearby? He had to search for her, scanning the knee-high grass before he found her in the pasture on the far side of Copper, curled up with her nose in a book. She could have been that girl in his memory, untouched by time. Or maybe that was the way his heart saw her.

Everything in this earthly world changed but one— he loved her. He had always loved her. He would forever love her.

He signaled Max, and the horse bolted forward. He rode into the falling twilight, glad for the shadows that hid him from sight.

Chapter Ten

"Dad and Justin are out with the sheriff," Addison explained as she grabbed a pancake from the stack on the table, rolled it around a sausage and a spoonful of scrambled eggs. "Dad's none too happy. Sheriff Todd refused to work on Sunday, which I understand, but it's frustrating. It's not like the town can afford a deputy or something to fill in."

"That's too bad. I hope the trail isn't too cold." Rori had heard Gramps's view before on the big-city sheriff. She finished browning the last batch of sausages for the Granger sisters and carried the fry pan to the table. "Your dad has to be worried about his cows."

"His pet cows." Cheyenne clarified as she tromped into the room, dressed to ride. All that was missing was a Stetson. "They're worth a good five or six grand a piece."

"Times are hard for a lot of people." Rori tipped the pan, rolling the links onto the paper towels. "It doesn't sound like a big band of rustlers."

"That's what we think, too." Autumn grabbed a

pancake and rolled up a to-go sandwich the way her sister had. "But we're riding patrols to be safe."

"We'll stay in cell range," Addison added, stepping into her boots in the mudroom.

"You'll have to man the main phone." Autumn snatched a travel mug and carried it to the coffeemaker. "I'll be back in time for Cady's appointment. In case she shows early, would you mind offering her coffee and giving me a jingle?"

"Will do." Rori considered the platters of food, largely untouched, on the table. Maybe she would plate up and keep breakfast warm in the oven for Justin and Frank so she could start cleaning the kitchen. "Which horse are you going to sell to her?"

"I'm hoping she and Misty will take a shine to each other." Autumn finished filling her mug, replaced the carafe and reached for the carton of coffee creamer. "I've been trying to find the right person for that mare for a long time. No one has been the right fit. For my other horses, sure, but not her. I'm hoping Cady is the right match."

"I guess we'll see. Misty is the palomino paint?"

"The most gorgeous horse ever, and sweet as the day is long. She doesn't just go to anyone." Autumn worried her bottom lip, protective of the horses she loved. "After I see Cady around horses, I'll know if I can trust her with Misty."

"No one understands the bond between a girl and her horse." Rori set the fry pan on a cold burner. "Not unless you've been there."

"That's right. It takes one to know one." She capped her thermos and headed toward the door. "My advice is to keep the coffee hot and fresh. My suspicion is that when Dad comes back, he's not going to be in a good mood."

"Thanks for the heads-up." Rori opened the dishwasher. "Maybe I'll bake blueberry muffins. He hinted they were his favorite."

"That would earn you big points with him." Autumn disappeared around the corner. "See ya later."

"Bye." Alone in the kitchen, she picked up two clean plates from the racks and carried them to the table. The picture window framed the backyard and half of the hillside perfectly. For as far as she could see foals pranced under the watchful eyes of their mothers in the nearby field and Buttercup, picketed on the back lawn, mooed and ran at Autumn as far as her generous rope would allow. When the heifer ran out of slack she tugged against her restraint with all her might, stretching her neck as far as it would go and then her long pink tongue toward Autumn's pancake rollup.

"You already have breakfast." Autumn's voice carried across the silent yard. "Sorry. You'll have to wait for Dad to spoil you."

Buttercup mooed pleadingly, sounding so pitiful Rori gathered a few molasses treats from a small bag in the mudroom. When she pushed through the screen door, the cow, bright-eyed as a puppy, ran straight at her. It was a little like looking a runaway train in the grill until the rope tautened. Buttercup skidded to a stop and danced in place, already knowing the treats were hers.

"You *are* the most spoiled cow ever."

Buttercup appeared to feel no remorse at this, so Rori held out one of the goodies on her palm. With a single swipe of that tongue, the treat was gone. The cow chewed it happily, jowls working.

"I'm glad you're here safe and sound." She patted Buttercup's neck. She hated to think what could be happening to the other missing cows. Where were they, and were they frightened? Being mistreated? Rori guessed that was what ate away at Justin and Frank. Sheriff Todd, whom she'd only seen at church, was from Detroit, and he might not understand the value of a farm animal, sometimes something that went far beyond their monetary worth.

She fed Buttercup the last treat and rubbed her poll. The cow's short coat felt bristly against her fingertips. Content, Buttercup flicked her tail and closed her eyes.

"What are you doing sweet-talking my best gal?" Frank called out across the yard.

Rori whipped around, unprepared for the sight of Justin on horseback riding in on the sun. He dismounted alongside his father and left the horses standing in the back yard.

"You've caught me red-handed." She cleared her throat, hoping her voice sounded unaffected. "I'm spoiling Buttercup."

"Like she needs more of that." Frank moseyed up to the cow, who batted her long curly eyelashes at him and pressed her forehead against his chest. "Thanks for it, though. You wouldn't still happen to have breakfast on the table?"

"And it's still warm."

"Bless you, girl. I'm so hungry I could eat my own boot." He gave the cow a final pat and broke away to the house, leaving her alone with Justin.

It was a total shocker he wasn't walking away from her. Nor was he doing his best to avoid her. Instead, he strode toward her with purpose. Larks sang in the nearby maple and Buttercup lowed a cheerful hello as the span of lush green grass separating them diminished. His shadow fell across her, and she shivered. Every step he took toward her felt as if it brought them closer to what could be.

You don't want a future with him, she told herself. She wasn't ready for him or anyone. Falling in love with him would be the biggest mistake. Hoping that he would love her in return was an even bigger mistake. All she could see was heartbreak brewing.

"That's nice of you to pamper Dad's favorite cow." Justin shoved his hands into his pockets, looking about as uncomfortable as she felt.

"It was my pleasure." She stroked Buttercup's nose. "What did the sheriff say?"

"Not much. He says because the trail is cold, there's no sense in trying to solve this thing. That we should collect the insurance money and get different cows."

"But those were special animals."

"Todd said a cow is a cow. His attitude might be the reason the town council is so unhappy with him." Justin shrugged. "Maybe they'll hire someone better come November, but in the meantime, we've got motorcycle tracks and hoof prints exiting our property near the main road. They could have loaded the cows into a trailer from there. Not a soul would have seen them. There are no other leads."

"Isn't the sheriff going to check with the auction houses? Maybe some of the county slaughterhouses?"

"He said he would, that's standard procedure, but I'm going to finish making the calls myself this morning. I don't trust him to do it fast enough. The cows were branded, so if they're found we have proof of claim. Other than that, there's nothing we can do."

"I'm sorry, Justin." She could read the strain and worry on his face and his concern for their animals. She fisted her hands to keep from reaching out to him. She didn't have the right to help smooth away the furrow in his brow or the tension tight in his jaw.

"In the meantime, we're going to start branding early." He tugged his hat brim lower to keep the sun out of his eyes. "That means we'll need you to haul the food out to us."

"Sure."

"Dad will give you the particulars. I just thought you might want a heads-up before you grocery shop." He stared down at the ground between them, kicking his toe into the thick grass. "We'll probably bring in more hired hands to keep an eye on things. That will mean more mouths to feed."

"It's all fine, Justin."

"Good." Did she feel torn up, too, remembering how it was to be close and knowing it could never be again? She sure didn't look it. He squared his shoulders, determined to seem at least as unaffected as she was. But one look at her hit him like a punch to the gut. He backed away. "It was good of you to coddle Buttercup. She's missing her cow buddies."

"Spoiling animals is my specialty." She brushed the cow's face one more time, her kindness revealed. Buttercup responded, her big brown eyes melting as she gazed up at her new friend. "Well, I've got to get back to work. Dishes are waiting in the sink and your breakfast is getting cold."

For a second he didn't realize she'd been speaking to him. He'd been so caught up in watching her lips move as she spoke, the gentle smile at the corners of her mouth, the innocence of sunlight on her creamy skin. Embarrassed that he'd been staring so hard at her, he nodded, his boots turning toward the back porch but his feelings and his spirit did not turn from her.

Her voice spoke to him from his memory, so strongly he could hear the babbling river and the leaves singing in the wind. *Tell me that we aren't going to change. That no matter what, it will always be you and me.*

Strange it was that God had brought her back home to Wyoming and at the same moment they'd needed a cook. Once, he would have believed that God had fated them to meet again. Now, he wasn't sure what God wanted from him, but surely it could not be to break him down to the soul over Rori one more time. There had to be a different answer.

He held the screen door for her, and Buttercup mooed her displeasure at being alone. When he glanced over his shoulder, the cow was straining at her rope in their direction. First chance he had, he intended to fix Buttercup's pasture.

"I think that heifer would come into the house if she could untie herself." Frank looked up from the table, a fork in hand. "Rori, I don't know for sure if that picket line will hold. You won't mind keeping an eye on her this morning, will you?"

"Not at all." She left Justin at the door, breezing away as if she had no clue what she did to him or how something deep in his soul leaned after her, wanting what could never be.

"You'll have to put her in the barn when you bring lunch out to us. Would you mind?" Dad cut into his pancake stack. "I'd do it, but I don't want to shut her up all day."

Justin noticed Rori didn't state the obvious. That Buttercup could be let out into the upper rangelands with the rest of the cattle or in with the expecting mares. He liked that she understood Buttercup was special to them all. The cow was used to being near the house.

"I don't mind at all. I'll lead her in with a trail of molasses treats." She went straight to the sink.

"You catch on quick. And I have to say, young lady, this is the tastiest breakfast I've had in some time."

"I'm glad you're happy." She turned on the faucet, looking like an image straight out of his long-ago dreams. Rori at his sink, in his kitchen, looking happy and relaxed and right where she belonged. Had he married, Dad would have given him this house. They would have lived here, been happy and raised their children here.

Why was he thinking of that now? Pain slammed into him like a spike to his chest and he put on the boot he'd just taken off. His stomach growled something fierce, so he grabbed a few pancakes and sausages off the table and headed straight out the door before any more foolish notions came to mind.

Rori Cornell had left him once. He had to believe she would do it again. Loving her or not had never made a whit of difference.

Buttercup spotted the food in his hand, mooed hopefully and then sadly when he bypassed her. He went straight to his horse, mounted up and put distance between him and Rori as fast as he could.

Cady Winslow adjusted her sunglasses. She'd stopped her SUV and glanced around. She saw nothing but a long ribbon of two-lane paved road behind her and stretching endlessly in front of her. There was no one else around, not unless you counted the hawk sitting on a telephone pole ahead, watching her with great interest.

She squinted at the directions Autumn had given her. She'd written them down carefully and followed them to the letter, but Cady had a terrible sinking feeling she was lost anyway. The fencing on one side of the road rising up to a rocky ridge had been going on for miles. Black cows glanced up from their grazing to stare at her. On the other side of the road, a field of something green and growing stretched as far as she could see. Huge metal wheels the size of semitruck tires were connected by pipes, spraying water onto the crops. Dozens of tiny rainbows glistened in the watery mist.

She checked the speedometer. She'd only gone nine miles, and the notes said a stone's throw past nine miles. How much was a stone's throw? Maybe she ought to go a little farther before she turned around. She felt like the only person in the entire county—there was nothing but silence and open space and the big bold sky. She was used to blasting horns and people everywhere and buildings crowding out the sky. Not for the first time did she have to wonder. Was she making a mistake?

Well, only time would tell. She'd left a secure job, her friends and family and nearly everything she knew to move to Wyoming. The right decision? It certainly was a scary one. She'd prayed over it, searched her soul and in the end she had followed her heart. Probably that wasn't very wise because in her experience, that's what brought a woman problems every time.

"Remember today's devotional," she told herself, holding on tight to the morning's verse from Proverbs she'd studied over breakfast at the motel's diner. *A man's heart plans his way, but the Lord directs his steps.*

She had to believe the Lord was showing her the way in the grand scheme, but for now she really needed to find the way to the Grangers' ranch. Why hadn't she sprung for the GPS option, she asked, and would it even work all the way out here?

The cows to her left bolted, running swiftly up the rising hill. Their sudden movement piqued her curiosity. What inspired cattle to run? Did they spot some sort of danger to them, or did they like to stretch their legs?

She had no clue, not until she spied a familiar man on horseback cresting the ridge. She recognized him, the man from the church parking lot. Frank Granger. Like a Western hero in the films she'd grown up on, he wore a black Stetson. With the brilliant blue sky framing him he looked larger than life, able to right wrongs and stay the distance.

If her pulse skipped three beats, she ignored it. Riveted, she could not take her eyes from him. He wore a white T-shirt and jeans, and he was the reason the cows were running. Tails up, they flocked to him like children to an ice-cream vendor and milled around his brown horse.

The man towered above them, hands reaching down to rub a nose here and the top of the head there. It was obvious the animals adored him. As if he felt her gaze, he looked up, the angle chased the shadow from his face and where sunlight touched it she saw high cheekbones, a straight nose and a handsome square jaw.

His hand shot up in a manly wave. As if he knew who she was—probably Autumn had told him she would be arriving—he gestured down the road and nodded.

Warmth rolled through her heart, a hint of awareness for this man she did not know. How embarrassing. She didn't have her hopes up, that was for sure! She waved her thanks, careful not to smile too much. She did not want her interest to show. She had gotten used to rejection over the past few years, when whatever bloom she'd had faded. She hadn't become as successful as she was without being a sensible, practical woman. So she swallowed a hint of disappointment and turned her attention to driving. She did not look into the side mirror for a chance to see him again. She kept her gaze firmly on the road and after it took a long curve, the driveway came into sight. Wooden fencing marched down the way and an overhead sign proclaimed, Stowaway Ranch.

Cottonwoods and maples shaded a lazy stream near to the driveway, and the gravel lane ribboned around a low hillside. It felt as if she were driving through a storybook picture as horses lifted their heads from grazing in an emerald-green meadow to watch her go by. A two-story house with brick and wood facing, a wide front porch and plentiful large windows crowned the rise, inviting her to come closer. Tree leaves tossed shade into the front yard, a porch swing rocked in the breeze and the white screen door opened as she pulled to a stop.

"You're right on time." Rori, whom she'd met at the church, smiled a greeting. Although she wore a simple cotton shirt and denim shorts with sneakers on her feet, she looked every bit as sweet. Cady knew if she'd taken a different path in her life, she would have a daughter about that age and hopefully one as nice.

Oh, these mid-life questionings were getting worse! Cady shut off the engine, left her purse on the seat and stepped out into the pleasant sunshine. She felt overdressed in her blouse and boot-cut trousers.

"I know Autumn is on her way in to meet with you. Would you like some coffee? Iced tea? Juice?"

"No, thanks. This is a lovely place."

"I think it's the prettiest property in the county, although I just work here." Rori breezed down the steps. "I live next door."

"Next door?" She laughed, glancing around. The horses that had been grazing were still watching her, obviously curious. As far as she could see there were no other buildings other than a large seven-bay garage tastefully set off to the side. There was not another house in sight. "You must mean the next ranch over?"

"Yes. My grandparents' farm isn't as grand as this, most spreads in these parts aren't." Conversationally, Rori led the way to a white picket fence and a gate, which she opened.

Cady gasped at the garden, where old-world lilac trees stood watch over canes of climbing roses. Cabbage roses that had grown taller than she was lined the fence, and miniature shrubs lined the pathway that skirted the side of the rather grand house. The wind lazily lifted the most delicious fragrance from the colorful blossoms.

Once, the walled garden had been grand, but now the blooms were in need of deadheading and the shrubs of a good trimming. Cady sighed down to the bottom of her soul. It reminded her of a garden she'd read about in a book when she'd been young. As a school girl she'd always had her nose in a book, to her mother's consternation.

"Here's Autumn now." Rori opened the far gate and led the way to an expansive backyard. The grass, neatly trimmed, was flawless except for the black cow with a white face who stood in the middle of it, mooing loudly.

"Buttercup, no one has forgotten you." Autumn paraded into sight, Stetson shading her face. "Hi, Cady. Sorry about Buttercup. She's rather loud. She's Dad's favorite pet cow."

Not that she'd ever heard of a pet cow, but she could certainly see the animal was used to attention. She'd never thought of cows as happy, but this one beamed dog-like joy with those bright eyes and smiling expression. Cady remembered the man on horseback swarmed by his cows. Frank Granger appeared to be such a strong man, capable and rugged, but obviously kind to animals and elderly ladies.

Very hard not to like that.

Chapter Eleven

"Dad?" Justin raised his voice. Maybe then his father could hear him, but Frank Granger seemed to be off in his thoughts. Maybe he was worried about his missing cows. Justin nudged Max up the rocky slope into the shade of a few sparse evergreens. The five hundred head of mother cows in this field ambled along with babies at their sides. Across the milling black and white herd, he spotted Cheyenne and Scotty, barely visible through the dust cloud rising up like smog.

"Dad!" He bellowed louder.

Up ahead, his father startled and twisted around in his saddle. "What is it, son?"

"You want to stop here?"

"What?" Frank looked around as if realizing where he was. Pretty strange, since he wasn't a man given to daydreaming. "Got a lot more on my mind than I figured. We'll stop for grub and then we'll separate the herd."

"Autumn should be back by then," he agreed. He was a good cutter, but the work went faster with Autumn at his side. "You want to take a break, Dad? Ride down to the house. Maybe call the sheriff again?"

"No." A sharp, quick answer, not at all laid-back Frank Granger's manner.

Wow. His father was agitated about something. But what? His first guess would be a woman, but that didn't make any sense. His father was an avowed bachelor.

Maybe he was projecting his own troubles, Justin wondered. He certainly did have a woman on the mind—Rori. And he couldn't stop wondering and remembering. Fortunately a cow darted from the herd with her little one at her side. He wheeled Max around. Something to take his mind off the woman. "Let's get 'em, boy."

Up to the challenge, Max dug in, lowered his head and roared down the grade, executing a perfect turn that cut off the cow's escape and drove her back to the herd. He hadn't been gone more than a few minutes at most, but Frank was still staring off into space.

Something was definitely up. Justin rode up to him. Once he'd reached the top of the ridge he realized that his dad wasn't staring off into space but down at the backyard. A mile away, it was nearly impossible to make out details, but a gray SUV was still in the driveway. The lodge lady come to buy the horse?

No, why would Dad be interested in a city woman? Justin dismissed that out of hand. Something else had to be wrong. It wasn't like Dad to keep things bottled up for long. He would talk about it in time. That was the benefit of being your father's best friend.

"Hey," he said, knuckling back his hat. "Want to ride down and fetch lunch?"

"No, Rori's on her way up. She's behind the trees. I saw her leave the house. We'll wait here for her because

I feel like staying put. Must be old age." Frank winked, back to his lighthearted, laid-back self.

"You're not so old, old man." A joke between them but it was soon forgotten when Rori rode into sight, appearing round the copse of trees.

She sat straight in her saddle, rocking gently with Copper's gait, talking to her horse and the horse she led, carrying the bundles of food and drink. By the look of things, she was enjoying whatever it was she was saying to the horses, chatting away as Copper nodded in agreement. She might look amazing in a dress and heels, but this was how he liked her best. With her hair pulled back in a ponytail and a ball cap shading her face, his country girl.

"Justin? Do you hear me, boy?"

He shook his head, unaware of how much time had passed. "What did you say?"

"Go down and help her, son." Understanding layered those words.

Justin blushed, aware his dad had known all along what he had just figured out. He whistled Max to a walk, cutting a path through the cattle to the gate. His sisters had dismounted and were giving a few calves their attentions. Maybe Cheyenne or Addison called out to him, he didn't exactly notice, because he couldn't take his gaze off Rori. She was still a fair distance away, far enough that her voice couldn't reach him. She drew him anyway, making him hunger for the melody of her words and her gentle presence.

Boy, am I in big trouble. He headed down the incline toward her, sure the grass was greener, the birdsong sweeter because of her. This moment was like a piece of the future he'd once wanted—the moment when she looked up and saw him riding toward her, the way she lit up with gladness and made his world brighter. He drank in the moment—the jingle of the bridle, the placid clomp of horse hooves and the Wyoming landscape stretching out all around them. His love for her lifted like hope on a prayer.

Lord, help me not to show it. You have to know this is a love that's not meant to be.

"Justin." She called across the closing distance. "Autumn said to tell you she's on her way."

"I take it things went well with the lodge lady?"

"Cady Winslow. Yep. She fell in love with Misty."

"Autumn must be glad." All he had to do was to play it cool, not be too remote or too interested, maybe frown a little and that ought to hide the fact that instead of taking the pack horse's lead from her, he wanted to take her hand in his like he used to do.

"She said she's been waiting for the right owner for Misty, and once I met the mare I knew why. Gorgeous."

Don't look at her, he told himself, staring as hard as he could at the ground ahead. If he didn't look, he wouldn't be captivated by the adorable way she tilted her head when she talked. He wouldn't be tempted to want to recapture the past, which was gone, or to wish for the soft warmth of her smaller hand in his.

"And sweet," Rori went on, talking about the horse, unaware that he was thinking the same thing.

Gorgeous. Sweet. So rare that he'd never felt the same way about another woman. Once, that had been why Tia had been so attractive to him because she hadn't held the power over his heart, she never could have claimed a part of his soul.

"Not that any horse is better than Copper, of course," she went on.

Copper snorted as if to say, "Of course."

"But Misty is definitely the second best."

"The third," Justin found himself arguing as Max nickered as if to say he was a touch insulted at being left out.

"Sorry, Max." Rori apologized and the gelding seemed satisfied. "You must miss riding Scout all day."

"It was a hard thing when he got too old for ranch work." He bowed his head, looking down instead of at her. "He started getting winded easily and dragging by day's end. It broke my heart to retire him, but I think he knew. He was ready."

"You miss him."

"We miss each other." He shrugged as if he wasn't troubled by anything as pesky as an emotion, but she wasn't fooled.

"He was down in the paddock watching me saddle up," she confessed. "He kept glancing up at the ridge. He knew you were up here. It nearly broke my heart to leave him behind. I gave him a handful of those treats he loves."

"Thanks. I'm sure he appreciated it. I know he gets lonely. He and I spent all day every day together for more years than I care to count."

"I know. I missed Copper when I was away. There wasn't a single day I didn't wish he and I were galloping through a field together or just sitting close reading while he grazed."

"Were you happy in Dallas?"

"It wasn't a bad life, but it was second best to life here."

"Are you sorry you left?" His question came quietly, hovering in the air between them like an undetonated bomb, one about to go off at anytime and destroy their tentative peace.

But it didn't. She heard a deeper layer to his question, one she'd never known before.

"No," she answered honestly. "I'm just sorry I didn't come back sooner."

They'd nearly reached the ridge, so he didn't answer and she stayed silent. As the horses plodded up the rocky trail, a hawk circled overhead, calling out as he sailed wide, hunting. The smaller birds went silent, disappearing from sight. Nothing but the wind moved the grasses as they circled toward the fence.

It felt comfortable riding quietly at Justin's side, like all the times they'd gone off together on horseback. She breathed in the fresh air, enjoying the companionable silence, God's nature spread out before her and the pleasure of Justin's company. All that was missing was the way he used to take her hand in his when they rode.

Some things were lost forever. She did not reach out to him but drew Copper to a halt. Justin rode up to open the gate, tall and confident in his saddle, a man who took her breath away.

No doubt about it. Justin had grown up into a fine man.

A man she could not let herself love.

She pressed her heels against Copper's side, urging him forward where Cheyenne and Addison were calling out welcomes to her, surrounded by adorable baby calves.

All afternoon long and into the evening the image dogged him, the one of Rori cuddling up to the calves. The delight on her face as the doe-eyed creatures gathered around her, eager for head pats and handfuls of grain the girls were giving out like candy. Her cheerful alto, the fun she seemed to be having, and how comfortable she looked among the animals. Not what he might expect from a girl who'd spent a significant chunk of time living an urban life.

She was just passing time until summer's end. They both knew it. She'd never said a word about staying. When she was back on her feet and recovered from the blow of her marriage falling apart, she would be off again, leaving him behind. He had to keep that truth front and center in his mind. He could not afford to forget it.

"That's the last one." Dad straightened up. "That's one herd tagged. We did good today, son."

"Desperation." He released the ropes hobbling the bleating calf, who scrambled to his feet crying for his mama on the other side of the sturdy fence. The desperate mother answered, mooing long and worried. She did not like being separated from her baby.

"That's all right, Moonshine. Your little guy is gonna be with you in a second." Dad rubbed the cow's nose and she quieted, anxious until he opened the gate just enough to let the calf leap through. Once reunited, the mother inspected her little one with great care.

Long day. Justin squinted at the sun low in the sky, tossed his hat onto a fence post and stretched his back. He hurt everywhere. They had moved up branding a month so the youngest cows wouldn't be vulnerable. A brand was proof of ownership. That wouldn't discourage any returning rustlers, but it would limit the way they could profit.

"I'm beat." Cheyenne dismounted, leading her cutting horse, Lulu, by the reins. "I spent all school year missing being here in a saddle on the back of my horse. But I forgot about these kinds of days."

"Makes you miss the classroom." Justin took a swig of his water. He was too hot for a swallow to make much of a difference, so he upended the bottle over his head. That was better. "I think we should leave the herd down here by the barn for the night. Run them back up come morning."

"Sounds like a plan. I'm going to go soak in the tub." Cheyenne limped away. "I hope Rori left us something good for supper."

"Not that it's probably still warm." Autumn rode up, streaked with dirt and sweat, wearing a wide grin. She was still in a good mood over selling her mare. "Or if Rori did leave food to keep warm in the oven, it's probably dry by now."

He hadn't seen her leave, and he'd been looking. But Copper wasn't in his stall. He hated that he'd missed seeing her.

He hated that he'd wanted to see her.

"I'll take care of the horses." Addison trotted up. "I got the easiest job today, so I don't mind. Justin, I'm taking Max."

"Thanks, Addy." He grabbed his hat, patted a cow straining through the slats of the fence, extracted the hem of his T-shirt from her mouth, and walked on aching feet to the barn. The hot breeze didn't help cool him one bit, and even in the shaded main aisle, sweat kept rolling down the back of his neck.

Scout nickered, running in from the paddock to his stall, head up, dark eyes hopeful.

"You want to take a ride, buddy?"

The one excited nicker said it all. Justin grabbed Scout's bridle from the tackroom. The thought of taking a swim in the river put a bounce in his step.

Rori knew she should be home weeding Gram's garden, but she'd had to escape. She needed fresh air to clear her head. The last thing she wanted to do was to expose her dear grandparents to more of her troubles. They thought she was doing well, and she wanted them to keep thinking that. They didn't need to waste time worrying about her. She'd made a mess of her life, but that was her problem. Besides, they had been completely enchanting together, sitting side by side in the old porch swing, chatting about the upcoming bake and rummage sale at the church. Gram was planning on baking her renowned angel food cake for the event.

"Looks like we're here, boy." She slid off Copper's bare back, her sneakers sinking into the fragrant grasses. Wildflowers dotted the small meadow with the brilliant yellows of dandelions and buttercups, the reds of Indian paintbrush and a few purple coneflowers.

Copper rubbed his head against her, an affectionate gesture, and she stroked her fingers through his mane. The hot wind lifted her bangs from her forehead and she lifted her face. That felt so good. The silence, the aloneness, the beauty all coalesced into perfection. She'd missed the realness of a life on the land.

If she had come back after college, would she have been happier? She didn't know, but the restlessness remained, unanswered questions that made her uncertain about the decisions she'd made in her life. She'd tried to follow where the Lord led, but maybe she'd been wrong. The package that had come in today's mail was proof enough of that.

The swimming hole looked the same as it always had. The water's melody, the thick knotted rope hanging from a sturdy maple bough, the feeling of solitude and peace were all just as she'd remembered it. Time stood still here. She felt as if she were eighteen again as she kicked off her sneakers and grabbed hold of the rope. Leaving her troubles behind, she pulled it as far as it would go, tightened her grip and took a leap, swinging out over the grassy bank.

Out of the corner of her eye she saw something big and dark breaking through the foliage. Adrenaline spiked through her as the ground fell away and water winked up at her. Copper tore one last mouthful of grass before his head shot up, scenting the intruder. She couldn't help him.

"Rori?" A familiar baritone rolled like thunder across the small clearing.

"Justin?" It was startling to see him riding out of the clutch of the shadows.

Her grip slipped, the rope slid between her palms, and the friction burned so she let go. The last thing she remembered was shrieking as she fell unprepared into the river below. She grabbed a bite of air just before water cascaded over her head and pulled her down.

What was *he* doing here? Hard and stoic Justin Granger was no longer the type to cannonball into a river. She kicked, sputtering to the surface and swam to the bank.

"Sorry about that." He towered over her, amusement relaxing the hard planes of the face she knew so well. "I didn't mean to startle you."

"Well, you did." Not the best comeback in the world, but she was startled. That had to be the reason why her brain wasn't functioning properly and *not* because he was standing before her looking like the best of blessings in a pair of cutoffs and a T-shirt advertising a rodeo. She said the first thing that popped into her mind. "I didn't know you were a bronco rider."

"No, but Tucker is. We always head over to Cheyenne

for the rodeo. The girls compete in the horse events."
He grabbed her elbow to help her up the bank.

His touch felt comforting, like coming home after a
long journey. Tension slid out of her muscles. This was
not exactly like old times, she realized as she landed in
the soft grass. Everything had changed between them,
even the way he looked into her eyes. Was it the lost past
she ached for? Or something else?

Don't think about that, she warned herself. She
feared the answer wasn't what she wanted it to be. She
shook her head, and droplets flew into the air. "Don't
tell me you came to play in the river?"

"What if I did? And there's a bigger question here.
Why are you on my family's land?"

"I figured the no-trespassing signs along the property
line didn't apply to me. They never have."

"You did notice the other signs. The ones that said
owner will protect with force?"

Oh, she spotted that twinkle of amusement he was
working so hard to hide. "Just try it, buster. Country girls
know how to hold their own."

"Is that so?" he challenged, grabbing her into his
arms before she could do more than squeal. He was
warm from the sun and smelled of hay and summer.
"Looks like you can't hold your own against me."

"I'm in a slight predicament, that's all. I could break
your hold easily, I'm sure." She was laughing too hard
to speak. "Justin, you aren't going to—"

"Take a deep breath," he interrupted as two quick
steps brought him to the bank's edge. The river burbled
below, swift and refreshing, and both horses watched
curiously as he rocked her toward the edge. "One."

"Don't you throw me," she told him.

"Two. It seems to me that you don't have much say-so." He held her safe against his chest, right where she belonged.

"You put me down this instant." She laughed, the past melted and there were no wounds between them, no breakup, no lost years, no regrets.

"Three." He swung her with care, launching her safely over the bank and out of his arms.

"Justiiin!" She squealed as the momentum of his toss sent her up into the air and then down, down toward the rippling waters.

A splash silenced her and when she disappeared beneath the river's surface he kicked off his shoes and joined her.

Chapter Twelve

"I can't believe you did that." She was waiting for him when he surfaced, swiping water out of her face and doing her best to look mad at him, which she wasn't. She had to bite the inside of her mouth to keep from laughing out loud. "What were you thinking?"

"That it would be fun to dump you in the river."

"Oh, and do you think this is fun?" She launched out of the water like a bouncing tiger, her hands landing squarely on his wide shoulders. She shoved hard enough to dunk him beneath the water. His dark hair swirled in the current before he disappeared.

Something snaked around her wrist and tugged. With a shriek she was hurled down beneath the surface, spitting water out of her mouth as she went. That Justin, he was grinning at her looking like ten different kinds of trouble as he took off down the river, holding her captive and carrying her with him.

Good thing she'd managed to get enough air! And if he thought she would go along for the ride, he was sorely mistaken. That Justin hadn't changed much, he was still as bossy as ever. She grabbed his hand holding her wrist and searched for the pressure point in his palm that would make him release her.

He knew what she was up to because his arms came around her, trapping her against his chest as he soared upward. They broke the surface, water droplets tickling like music all around them.

"Ha!" Justin laughed. "Try to get away from me now."

"I'm sure I could if I wanted to." In truth she was stuck, caught like a fish on a line, and her heart was, too.

Water clung to her lashes, framing the edges of her view like light through diamonds. Although the current was carrying them away, she felt safe in his arms. He was her champion, a man who chased away her every sadness and all her regrets. Her pulse skipped a beat. Her entire being stilled.

His gaze dropped to her mouth and lingered, as if he felt this, too. Did he want to kiss her, or was he simply remembering how amazing their kisses had been?

Please kiss me. The wish lifted like a prayer from her soul. Was there a way to recapture the past? Her beliefs in true love had shattered, her trust that love could last, but in his arms, in the moment, gazing into the midnight blue of his eyes, she began to hope.

He ripped away from her. Answer enough. She floated freely on the current, but he put a hand to her back and kept her from drifting away. She stayed at his side, treading water, feeling the push of the current, the inexorable pull of what could be.

"I don't want Copper thinking I've taken off with you." His explanation was a thin one.

She didn't comment. Instead she took after him,

keeping her head above water and swimming at a diagonal against the river's force.

"I didn't know you still came up here," she said when they'd reached the bank. "I would have thought your playing in the river days were behind you."

"Now and then I have a rough day and I feel the need."

"You don't normally brand the calves for another month."

"We'll have to de-horn, vaccinate and cut them then. Doubles the work." He offered his hand to help her up the bank. "I should have spent the day in the fields in the air-conditioned tractor."

"Sounds like a better chore, as long as your iPod is charged." She laid her palm on his, ignoring how familiar it felt to let him help her up the rocks and onto the cushiony grass.

"Are you kidding? We have satellite radio and a stereo system to keep me grinning even on a long day." The horses continued to graze side by side in companionable silence, friends catching up.

"You rode Scout," she noticed.

"Just like old times."

"Yes." She could almost believe nothing had really changed. Did he feel this, too, the push of the future, the pull of the past? The earth was springy beneath her bare feet, the ground radiating the sun's warmth and her spirit as light as a nearby lark's song. She felt whole, as if grace and not the wind breezed over her.

"You never said what you were doing here." Justin pulled back the rope as leaves rustled a quiet symphony. "A tough day for you, too?"

"Not at work, if that's what you're asking."

"It crossed my mind. It's a lot of work keeping care

of us all. Only my aunt Opal would do it and she did it out of love, because we were family."

"You all feel like family to me." She blushed, realizing too late what she'd said.

"What happened today?" He stepped back, allowing her room to step in and take the rope.

"I received my divorce papers." She curled her hands around the thick hemp, holding on tight. "I sign on the designated lines and acknowledge the biggest failure of my life."

"It can't be the biggest." He felt her sadness as if it were his own, and he hated that she was hurting. "Wasn't turning me down your biggest mistake?"

"Some people might think so, but I'm not one of them." At least she could still crack a joke.

"You're right. I should have waited for you." The admission killed him because a man never liked to be wrong, but it was time he lowered his pride and let in the truth. "I never even thought of it. I shouldn't have made my proposal all or nothing. Proof I wasn't ready to be a husband."

"I wasn't ready to be a wife." Pain filled her. He knew, because it was his, too.

"And when you were ready, it wasn't with me." He swallowed against the rising tide of emotions too strong to name, ones he did not want to bear. "What happened to your marriage?"

"I wanted kids, he didn't. I wanted to focus on our marriage, he wanted to focus on his career. I wanted to move out of the city and live on a little acreage, he wanted to stay near his country club."

"You wanted different things." His parents were like that and it had torn them apart.

"Yes, and one day the differences were too great and he no longer wanted me."

"How could any man not want you?" Unbelievable. He couldn't imagine it.

"Brad decided he had more in common with his receptionist and surprised me by having the locks on the house changed, canceling my cards and moving all the money out of our joint bank accounts." Humiliation. She tried to hide it from him with a careless shrug.

Was he fooled? Not a chance. He brushed a wet tangle of hair away from her cheek and laid his hand there, his palm curved against the delicate line of her jaw and cheek. Tenderness, an emotion he'd long ago banned from feeling, ebbed through him, gentle and sweet and powerful enough to drown him.

"I'm sorry, Rori." He truly was. "You didn't deserve that."

"It's not so bad to start over. It's turned out all right. I haven't been this happy in a long time."

"Marriage is hard, and the wrong marriage is harder." His dad had always said this, and Justin had seen it with his own eyes. "There's something to be said for being single."

"Especially when you aren't the kind of woman a man will give everything for." She winced, as if she believed that. She blushed, as if she'd confessed too much.

Not to him. Never to him. He curled his hand to the back of her neck and drew her against his chest. Caring roared through him like the leading edge of a twister, but he couldn't let it devastate him. He had to be strong. He had to hold on to his resolve.

"Don't think there was anything missing in you." He

wanted her to know the truth. "The right man would give up anything for the privilege of loving you."

"Oh, Justin. You said exactly what my heart needed to hear." Her arms wrapped tight around his ribs, holding on tight, as if she hadn't had anyone to steady her in a long, long time.

His arms went around her, too. He wasn't ashamed to be the shoulder she needed to lean on, her soft place to fall and if only for this moment in time. He leaned his cheek against the crown of her head, breathing in the fragrance of her hair and the faint scent of strawberry shampoo. Immeasurable emotions threatened to break down the dam he'd put up.

Please, Lord, let those walls hold. Since I can't help loving her, at least don't make me feel it.

He wasn't too sure if the Lord could help him with that, but he prayed anyhow. Disaster was coming on the road ahead, there was no doubt about that. Hadn't Rori just told him that she was starting over? That she was ready to build a new life for herself? Obviously that would be back in Dallas.

"Now that I've all but cried on your shoulder." She tilted her head back, searching him as if she wanted to see his truths buried within. "Why haven't you let some woman snatch you off the market?"

"Because this woman I was seeing a few years back, Tia was her name." He released Rori so she wouldn't be as close, so that maybe he could try to hide from her how disillusioned he'd become. "We were talking on the phone, like we did every evening after I'd get in from the fields. She had another call and she put me on hold to take it. Except she didn't put me on hold. She must have hit the wrong button because the line didn't switch over."

"Uh-oh. That doesn't sound good."

"No. The next thing I heard her say was, Oh, Sarah, thank goodness you called. I'm on the phone with Justin. He bores me to tears and if he wasn't worth millions of dollars…" He took a breath, but the bad taste lingered. "That's when I broke in and told her we were done."

"I'm sorry she hurt you." Sincere, she laid a hand over his chest.

"I cared just enough about her to wind up bitter, but not more." His pulse beat betrayingly. Could she feel it? Would she guess that he'd never truly loved anyone but her? No matter how hard he'd tried, his heart kept circling back to her. "That's when I decided to stop dating. I've been good with it, but Dad suffers."

"Your father wants you to be happy. Sometimes happiness and marriage go hand in hand."

"Sometimes." His hand covered hers, tenderly. "My guess is that it's killing Dad. No grandkids. Autumn scares away every eligible bachelor."

"She scares them away? She's not frightening."

"No, but there have been men stopping by and I see at first their interest. But the minute they see her rope an animal, or work a horse or once we had the new farrier drive up during shooting practice, that's it. They are no longer interested. Cheyenne's got school to finish, and Addison, you've heard her views on marriage, I'm sure."

"She's pretty vocal about it."

"That leaves Tucker. He's competing on the rodeo circuit and always on the go. We hardly see him as it is. He's not going to settle down. Dad's never going to get those grandkids he wants."

"Poor Frank." She tried to move her hand, but he held it firmly, as if he didn't want to let her go. "But you can never know what the Lord has in store for you. Things might change. Autumn might find a man who doesn't scare easily. Cheyenne will finish school. Addison could meet someone who changes her mind."

"Tucker might come home," he finished.

"And you might lose your bitterness."

"Then we had all better pray for a handful of miracles because that's the only way those things are going to happen." He hated the bitterness that had built over the years, because he had let it. He could feel it now, dark the way a storm brewed on the horizon, threatening to take over until everything was dark. Until he'd driven everything away.

Rori was like the sun shining into his world, pushing back the clouds. And as much as he needed her, he could not lean on her. He could not count on her. With her hand, so small compared to his, resting on his chest, he wondered if she could feel how much he loved her. How much he wanted to draw her into his arms again and kiss her with all the tenderness he possessed, the way he used to do long ago under the shade of these very trees.

Should he do it? Everything inside him wanted to reach out to her, ask her to stay in Wild Horse and choose him this time around. But he let go of her and reached for the rope, swinging forgotten beside them, and offered it to her.

"Ladies first," he said.

Chapter Thirteen

The Greasy Spoon rang with noise and busyness, so Rori suggested taking their after-supper milkshakes to go.

"Good idea," Autumn said as they pushed through the queue at the entrance, where folks were standing to wait for a booth—a rarity in Wild Horse. "I guess this year's Frontier Days are off to a booming start."

That was an understatement. The festival used to be a small celebration over a single weekend, culminating in a local rodeo. But now the event had grown into an impressive affair with folks coming out from Jackson to join in the fun. Colorful vendors' booths lined the main street through town, closed off to traffic. Crowds of people milled from booth to booth admiring everything from branding irons to crocheted blankets to hand-blown glass. The scent of cotton candy and roasting hot dogs filled the air as kids dashed by, calling out to their parents.

At the hitching post, Copper raised his head as if trying to catch her attention. He looked worried. Maybe all the noise was bothering him.

"I've got to check on my buddy," she told Autumn,

turning her back on the temptation of the booths full of things to buy.

"It is a little loud," Autumn agreed, coming with her. "We could tie him down by the feed store. It looks quieter there."

"Just what I was thinking. I'll see if he's all right first." Rori took a sip of her milkshake. "Ever since Monday he's been dragging."

"Have we been working him too hard? You could use any of our horses to bring out meals to us."

"I know, but I think it would break his heart if I did that. Right, fella?" She laid a hand on his flank before she circled behind him.

He nickered, sounding as if he were in need of a little sympathy.

"I know how hard that is," Autumn agreed, running a hand along her mare's coat. They met at the hitching post, both separating the extra cups from their milkshakes. "I am very blessed to have the horses I do. I love everyone, but there's something special about a girl's first horse. There's something special about you, Bella."

The mare nodded, tossing her platinum forelock and mane.

"Very special," Rori agreed, laughing when Copper nibbled a kiss to her check. "I got your favorite. Strawberry."

"They aren't spoiled at all," Autumn quipped, pouring half her milkshake into the second cup. Bella was already lipping the rim, anxious for the treat.

"Not one bit," Rori agreed, holding the cup for Copper. He dipped his tongue into the icy drink, lapping it up hungrily. She leaned against the hitching post, enjoying the moment. There was so much to savor. The light shadow of dust in the air, the stunning blue sky and the milling sounds of people talking and laughing and having a good time. Above all the noises, one stood out from all the others. The faint steady gait of a certain cowboy.

"Why am I not surprised?" Justin asked, shaking his head at Copper's milkshake mustache. "I was going to call you, but when I thought about it I knew right where to find you."

"What are you doing here?" Joy rippled through her at the welcome sight of him strolling closer. "I thought you hated all this fuss and the crowds."

"I do, but I figured I might make an exception this year and check things out. Isn't that what we agreed to?" He sidled up to her at the post. The old wooden bar groaned a hint when he leaned on it. His elbow brushed her shoulder as he relaxed at her side. "Autumn, don't say one word."

"I'm doing my best to hold it back, but no guarantees," came the amused answer from the other side of Bella.

Out of the corner of her eye, Rori saw Autumn grinning wide, but she remained silent, working on the last of her milkshake.

"There's Dad." Justin inclined his head. "He got sidelined by Martha again."

Rori craned her neck to see around Copper. Sure enough, the gregarious, pleasantly plump Mrs. Wisener chattered away at Frank in front of the engraved horseshoe stand, clutching one of his shirtsleeves to keep him from getting away.

"Poor Dad," Autumn sympathized. "Should I go over and rescue him?"

"Someone better," he answered. As Autumn gave Bella a final pat, held out her hand for Copper's empty cup, and left with the *clip, clop* of her sandals, Justin crossed his arms over his chest. "She's probably trying to get him to join the town council. She's been lobbying hard and she doesn't want to take no for an answer."

"Why didn't you offer to go drag him away from her?" she wanted to know.

"Because I was afraid she would give up on Dad and decide to try angling me into the job. Can you see me as a politician?"

"No." She threw her head back and laughed merry and bright, her golden hair dancing in the wind.

"Well, you don't have to laugh so hard. It's not that funny."

"Sure it is."

"I happen to disagree."

"I hate to break it to you, but I can't see you sitting indoors and still for the length of a town meeting. I can't see you listening patiently to everyone's point of view," she quipped breezily. "You would hate it."

"True, I'm a man with flaws. But I'm improving." Oh, that interested her. He could see her light up. "If you stick around, you might see just how much."

"Maybe I've noticed." She rubbed her free hand over Copper's nose.

She noticed? That put a good feeling square in the center of his chest. For the past few days he'd been trying to put less importance on their meeting at the old swimming spot, but he couldn't do it. The evening had been stellar, a memory emblazoned upon his soul. And tonight, with the soft light of the sun casting across her like gold, she could be a princess with her country-girl charm and timeless beauty—that's what she would always be to him.

"You were right." Rori leaned closer conspiratorially, bringing with her the scent of strawberry milkshake and fabric softener. "Martha looks like she's trying to recruit Autumn for the job."

"I was smart to avoid that woman." He laughed. He hadn't expected Autumn to get roped in for the cause, but it looked as if she were extricating herself all right. She tugged Dad away, shaking her head politely. Neither of them looked as if they could escape fast enough.

"Woo-wee." Frank kept his voice low, but swept off his hat and rubbed at a few beads of sweat. "That woman knows how to put on the pressure. I was going to grab a bite a Clem's, but it's packed. Son, I was going to offer to buy you a hot dog, but it looks like you've found better company."

"Yes, but I'm not sure if I'm going to keep him," Rori quipped. The wind tossed a lock of gold across her face.

It took all his willpower not to push it out of her way. Once, touching her had been his right. Caring for her, letting her know how he felt, that was his to do. But no longer. Sorrow hit him hard, and he hoped it didn't show as he added his own teasing line. "Did you hear that, Dad? You might be stuck with me after all. If I hang with you, I'm bound to hurt your image."

"That you will, boy."

"I was just about to check out the branding iron booth." With a wink, Autumn patted Bella. "Dad, did you want to come with me?"

"Sure. You're a mite better for my reputation." Frank winked, donning his Stetson and joining his daughter. "I look like a good father when I'm with you."

"And what about me?" Justin asked above the round of laughter.

"I'll let my reputation take a hit," Rori offered. "I don't mind being seen with the likes of you. *Too* much."

"Good to know." He might be laughing, too, but he recognized the steady message in her eyes, the quiet connection that had always existed between them.

"Then you've got me," he told her. What he didn't tell her was that she had him for tonight or forever. It was her choice.

"Where do you want to go first?"

"I want to check out the pottery booths. Gram needs a new butter dish." She gave Copper a final pat, studied him carefully as if to make sure he was all right, and then held out her hand.

Nothing felt more right than twining his fingers through hers. Nothing felt more like a blessing than having her at his side.

"Look at Justin and Rori."

At his daughter's words, Frank set down an iron, glanced down the way and spotted his son in front of a bright red awning. Hard to see much, since Justin's hat brim was down, shading his face, but he knew his boy and he knew the signs. The way he leaned toward Rori, protected her from the passersby and watched her as if she were the most precious thing on earth. It all meant one thing.

"Seems to me they're havin' a good time." He cleared his throat and hoped that his prayers for his son weren't showing.

"Are you kidding?" Autumn stepped away from the stand. "It looks like old times. Remember?"

He did. He'd been still grieving Lainie when Justin had started dating the girl. Back then Rori had been a timid thing, but she had fit right in with the family as time went by. It was happening all over again, and he was thankful to the Lord for that. Justin was almost back to himself, and Frank saw hints of the man Justin was meant to become. Rori was good for him.

"Do you think she'll stay?" Autumn asked.

"Why wouldn't she?"

"Oh, she might want a job where she can use her music degree."

"We like music. She could play our piano."

"Yeah, but that might not be the same as at an actual school." Autumn dodged the crowd, zeroing in on some stand with jewelry. "Maybe this time Justin won't blow it."

"We can hope and pray." He did every night for Justin's happiness, as he did for all his kids. He loved them. He'd do anything for them. It killed him that he couldn't pave their way to a fulfilling future. Had he failed them? He'd married the wrong woman, or so time had proved in the end, and everyone had paid the price for it.

"Maybe love will be enough." Autumn's words were more of a question than a statement. She was a good girl, strong in all the ways that counted, and she had a tender spirit. It was showing now.

Sure, he knew what she was asking. If love could be enough. Frank shrugged. It sure hadn't been in his case. "I hope so, sweetheart."

He jammed his hands in his pocket, waiting while she checked out shiny crystals and polished stones on display. Folks milled around them like a river's current around a rock, always streaming. Across the way, Justin put his hand on Rori's back as they walked along. The girl was laughing and his son looked happy.

Happy. That's all he'd ever asked of the Lord. Frank

nodded, filling with an intense hope he hadn't felt in a long time. He hadn't been a hope-filled man in a long time. Right there was proof that God did work out all things for the good. A man just had to be patient.

"Oh, look, there's Cady." A plastic shopping bag crinkled as Autumn rolled it and jammed it into her pocket.

"Cady?" His heart slammed to a halt in his chest as he spotted her sauntering their way. The woman was grace personified. Her light brown hair was down, framing her face in a sleek bouncy way. She looked like a catalog page come to life.

"Autumn." A smile of pleasure changed the city woman from beautiful to stunning. She began weaving through the crowd with speed and intention.

"Oh, Dad, you have to meet her."

Before he could escape or at least think of a decent excuse to stay behind, Autumn caught him by the wrist and tugged. He stumbled forward, his pulse drumming so hard his blood pressure had to be in the red zone. He didn't want to meet the woman because he didn't want to see her reaction to him—maybe a quiet dismissal or a tactful lack of eye contact. Whatever it was, she wasn't going to feel this way for him, a country boy who spent his days with cattle and horses.

"Cady, this is my father, Frank Granger." Unaware, Autumn plunged ahead as if eager to introduce him.

Might as well make the best of it. He tipped his hat. "Nice to meet you, ma'am."

Here it comes, he thought. Brace yourself. He waited the split second it took for the woman to really look at him. He might be fit for his age from a life of hard work, but he had to be honest. He wasn't in the same league as she was used to. The sun had weathered him—

not bad, but not good either. He came with a lot of baggage—five kids, five hundred thousand acres and a failed marriage. His best friends were his children, his horse and his cows. Plus, he didn't have a fancy education. There hadn't been time for college, only the hard work of running a ranch and raising his family.

He figured Cady Winslow would see all this in an instant, give him a tepid but polite greeting, and focus back on his daughter. It sure would have been less painful to have avoided her, just as he'd done on the ridge the other day. He didn't think women like her would understand that his baggage and shortcomings were what he was proud of most.

"Nice to meet you." Her smile brightened. She met his gaze and held out her hand.

She had the prettiest green eyes. They could make the world's finest emeralds look dull. The impact of her gaze hit like lightning. Her hand felt fragile in his, delicate and refined and so soft, she had to be a dream.

"Good to meet you." His voice sounded strained, and he prayed to high heaven he wasn't blushing.

"Your daughter has told me all about you." She withdrew her hand, speaking quietly and a little rushed.

Maybe he made her uncomfortable. It wouldn't be the first time. He knew he was a big man, rough-and-tumble-looking, his hands scarred and callused from a lifetime of ranching. "I hate to think what she'd told you."

"Only good things," Cady assured him, as Autumn rolled her eyes.

"I told her I have the best dad. When I was ten, he bought me a champion quarter horse. Bella cost more than our house was worth at the time." Autumn didn't pause when surprise passed over Cady's face. "I competed throughout high school. That's how I earned money for Misty's mother."

"Everyone has told me what a fine horse I'm getting. I thought she was lovely," Cady explained. "I did some research because I wanted to understand about pedigrees and her parents and the kind of rating that she has. She's amazing. I'm so excited to start riding her."

"Do you know where you want to board her?" Autumn asked.

Glad the women were engaged in conversation, he could simply drink in the sight of Cady Winslow, bask in the gentle melody of her voice and wish—just a tad—for her. Not that she could be interested in him. But she hadn't dismissed him either. That spoke well of her character.

"Hey, Dad." His middle daughter popped up at his side. "I wanted to meet Cady."

"You must be Cheyenne." The woman held out her hand pleasantly, looking pleased to meet the girl.

Now that surprised him. Maybe she was that way with everyone. That had to be it. The sinking sensation in his chest made no sense. It couldn't be disappointment. He'd only been doing a little wishful thinking and nothing more. It was a fact he couldn't get tangled up with a city girl.

"Oh, and before I forget." Cady reached into her slim, fashionable shoulder bag and pulled out a folded-up check and held it out to Autumn. "This is for you. Misty is now officially mine. I'm so thrilled."

"So am I." Autumn pocketed the check without looking at it. "You two are perfectly matched. She needs someone as gentle and quiet as she is. She's sensitive. Don't worry, I'll go over everything you need to know."

"And I'll take notes. I want to do this right." She

clasped her hands with excitement. "My contractor tells me the fence will be the last to go up, so it doesn't get knocked down accidentally by the heavy equipment they are bringing in. I think the wait will about kill me."

"I'll e-mail you a list of the best places to board," Autumn promised. "And I include free delivery, so if you don't want to go with us I totally understand. I'll trailer Misty wherever you want."

"I promise to let you know as soon as I decide. I'm juggling a lot between the remodeling and the move."

"How is that going?" he broke in.

"I hired the Wiseners' son. He came with the best references and a fair price for the work." Nerves fluttered in her stomach. The man was even more handsome close up.

"It must be hard to know who to hire when you don't know folks in the area." His deep voice rumbled with a blend of strength and kindness. "Seems like you did everything right. The Wisener boy does good work."

"I'm relieved to hear that for sure." It was such a big project. So much could go wrong.

But that wasn't the reason the flutters in her stomach went from butterfly to buffalo-size. Her years working her way up from junior associate to full partner in one of the best personal injury firms on the East Coast had taught her to handle her nerves. Yet standing before Frank Granger had her knees knocking. Good thing she was wearing jeans so it wasn't noticeable.

She couldn't ever remember wanting a man to like her before. Not like this. The deepest places within her heart ached for the sight of his smile and prayed to see a light of interest in his lapis-blue eyes. She knew full well it was foolish of her, but a tiny flare of hope filled her anyway.

"I told Autumn I was impressed by your family's

ranch." Self-conscious, she slipped her hands into the front pockets of her jeans, trying to hide them. "I've never been on a working ranch before. It was interesting."

"Glad you thought so." He said it politely enough, but he said nothing more. He didn't directly meet her gaze but looked a little past her right ear.

She could have told him that when she'd petted Buttercup staked in their yard it was the first time she'd been so close to a cow, or her trip to his ranch was the first time she'd ever stepped foot inside a horse barn. She'd been entranced by the foals, how Wildflower had allowed her to stroke her baby through the fence, and how wonderful it must be to live in such a beautiful, vibrant place.

She *could* have said all those things, but she kept silent. Perhaps he wasn't interested in what she had to say. He clearly didn't seem interested in her.

"I don't want to keep you from your family time." She backed away, praying to the Lord above that she was adequately hiding her disappointment. "I'll be in touch, Autumn."

"You don't have to go. You could hang with us." She was such a nice girl, but was that sympathy in her voice?

Cady truly hoped it wasn't. She couldn't bear it if anyone had guessed her feelings. She didn't let herself hope very often, and she had been wrong to do so tonight.

"Thank you, but I have plans." She pasted on what should pass for a smile. "It was nice meeting you, Cheyenne and Frank."

"It was great meeting you," Cheyenne enthused. "You and I will have to get together. I want to go over some basic veterinary care, just things you should know and stuff to watch out for. Since this is your first horse and all."

"That's nice. I would appreciate that very much."

She swallowed hard when Frank tipped his hat to her. That was all—no word of goodbye, nothing—before he led his daughters away. She forced her feet to carry her forward to the next vendor and stood unseeing at the booth's contents, trying to calm the ache in her soul.

That's what a woman her age deserved, she feared, for wishing as if she were young again, wanting a young girl's dreams. Love had passed her by in life, she had to accept it. She set her chin and the electric branding irons in front of her came into focus. She'd learned the hard way you could not live your life looking backward. The past was gone. Only the present mattered.

She thought of her morning's devotional verse. *This is the day the Lord has made; we will rejoice and be glad in it.* Those comforting words strengthened her as Tim Wisener Junior's wife called out to her, rushing over to say a friendly hello.

Chapter Fourteen

"What was that?" Autumn demanded, her voice pitched low so that it wouldn't carry, but Justin heard it. She was coming closer through the crowd, looking upset. She skidded to a stop at a stand showcasing hand-woven horse blankets. "Dad, you were rude to Cady."

"Yeah, Dad. Totally rude," Cheyenne agreed.

"No, I just didn't have much to say." Frank's color was high, as if he was mad or upset. A muscle ticked along his clenched jawline.

What was going on? Justin pulled his wallet out of his back pocket and tossed two twenties onto the table.

"Justin, what do you think you're doing?" Rori shook her head, scattering locks of honey and gold. "I can't let you pay for this."

"Just try to stop me." He took the aqua-blue blanket the sales lady had folded and bagged.

"You're spoiling me." She might be protesting, but her eyes said she appreciated it. When Rori was like this, her worries forgotten, her guards down, she took his breath away.

"A little spoiling won't hurt you." He kept his tone low, hoping his family couldn't hear, but he knew that was a pointless hope. Both of his sisters were grinning ear to ear and even Dad looked a little less upset at seeing them together.

"I saw you talking to Cady." Rori turned to Autumn. "Was that a check she gave you? Is the big sale official?"

"Yes. No buyer's remorse with her. I like that about her." Autumn patted her pocket where the check resided safely. "Plus, it was a personal check for forty thousand dollars. She didn't even haggle."

"That's class," Rori agreed. "She really must want Misty."

"I think it was love at first sight," Autumn answered, her voice low, shoving past him to talk with Rori. "I didn't want to take advantage of Cady, so I had to make sure she wasn't just carried away by the idea of owning a horse. It happens to a lot of people."

Dad's face was redder than ever, and he took a sudden intense interest in a pink horse blanket. What were the chances he didn't even see what was directly in front of him? And why did the girls talking about Cady Winslow seem to upset him? Justin glanced over his shoulder, searching the crowds for the woman. There she was, chatting with Tim Junior and his wife. She was elegant and friendly and if Autumn would sell one of her favorite mares to her, she had to be a good person. Autumn checked references extensively. Could his dad like the lady?

No. Impossible. Dad hadn't shown any interest in dating since they'd buried Mom. Justin accepted change from the vendor and pocketed it. What was bothering his dad? Maybe the missing cattle was troubling him more than he'd let on.

Dad jerked away from the blanket, realizing the color at last, and hurried to catch up with them.

"Is Frank all right?" Rori leaned in, concern layered in her hushed tone. "He seems distracted."

"Must have a lot on his mind." And maybe it was Cady Winslow, after all. He caught his dad looking at the far end of the street, past the crowd, to where the two women were chatting. Cady Winslow lifted her hand in a wave and left the Wiseners behind, heading down the street into the setting sun. The long low rays of light seemed to swallow her and, judging by the look on his father's face, Frank Granger had never seen a more beautiful sight.

Now that was interesting.

"You rode Scout?" Rori had only seemed to notice the bay gelding at the far end of the hitching post. A good two dozen animals stood drowsing in the shade all waiting for their owners.

"I always ride him in the evenings. Dad drove, but I didn't ride with him because I'd promised Scout a trip to town." What he didn't say was that he'd hoped to ride along with her home. The lowering sun, the warm evening, the privilege of her company sounded like a mighty fine way to pass the time. Just so she wouldn't guess how much it meant to him, he kept his tone off-hand. "Scout and I might as well keep you company, since we're all heading the same way. If you wouldn't mind hanging with us."

"I suppose Copper and I could tolerate it." She sparkled up at him, brilliant and precious. Every moment spent in her company made him want to believe in happily-ever-afters and second chances. But did she feel the same way? She didn't appear to be. Unaffected, she sauntered beside him, her stride relaxed and easy, her hand brushing his to take the shopping bags he was carrying for her. "It would be nice to ride home with you."

The link between his heart and hers strengthened until he could feel what she did not say. The evening had been like a gift, one he'd never figured on having again. Maybe she didn't either.

This isn't a second chance, he reminded himself. He couldn't assume that it was. He laid a hand on Copper's flank, letting the animal know who was standing behind him, and held open the leather flap on Rori's saddlebag. She carefully packed her purchases inside, and he took the time to adore her. The slope of her perfect nose, the smiling shape of her lips, the tiny cleft in her chin that was impossible to see unless he was kissing close. He knew her so well, he'd dreamed of her face every night when he knelt down to pray. Could things change? Could they make this their second chance?

Please fall in love with me, he pleaded. Not that she would. Not that he could trust her again if she did. But he wanted nothing more than a future with her, one he could not let himself see. He caressed a stray curl from her forehead, just so he could be closer to her.

Goodbyes rang out. He hardly noticed. Rori was the center of his world. She was all he could see, all he knew. Vaguely he was aware of Dad heading off toward the truck he'd parked on a side street, saying he'd best get home and check on Addison, since she'd offered to stay and keep an eye on the last mare about ready to foal.

Cheyenne and Autumn mounted up and trotted away. The clatter of steeled hooves on blacktop faded. His pulse pounded and pattered, because he was alone with Rori. The thinning crowd, the vendors beginning to close up for the night, the other horses drowsing nearby hardly existed for him as he untied Copper's reins from the post.

Rori hopped up and settled into her saddle, no longer just the girl he remembered, but so much more. A woman of substance and beauty, gentleness and grace, laughing as she chatted to Copper, who reached around to lip her ankle affectionately, glad to see her. With her ball cap shading her face, her hair dancing in the wind, she made him believe. She chased away the bitterness within him and he saw promises of long-lost dreams. If he could spend his days at her side, simply serving her, then he could ask for nothing more.

"Hurry up. Copper and I are ready to roll." She'd come alive, no longer sad and lost, more confident than he'd ever seen her. Gently, she reined Copper around, the old horse chipper, too. He arched his neck, showing off for his mistress, and the pair launched forward, not bothering to wait.

"You had better hurry up, Justin," she called over her shoulder. "Catch us if you can."

He loved her just like this, the Rori he'd never seen before. Strong and sure, she rode off like the wind, impossible to fence in, golden hair flying behind her. Away she went, his heart.

Scout stomped his hooves, anxious to step up to the challenge. Not one to be left behind either, Justin loosened the knotted reins, swung into the saddle and gave the gelding his head. With a flick of his tail, Scout was off, plunging down the street, ears back, churning into a smooth, swift gallop. Town rolled away behind him, and he moved Scout onto the dirt shouldering the road and crouched low, urging Scout faster.

Up ahead, Rori glanced over her shoulder, spotted them

and drew her gelding to a walk. She twisted around in the saddle. "Copper and I decided to give you a break. If we didn't stop, you would never be able to catch up with us."

"We were making good progress," he quipped. "Seems to me you stopped before we could show you two up."

"Let's call it a draw."

"Deal." As he caught up to her, Scout and Copper touched noses, old friends exchanging sentiments. "Thanks for coming along with me tonight."

"It was my pleasure. It's been a long time since I've enjoyed a small-town street fair. Especially in the presence of such a handsome guy."

"Why, thank you." He winked.

"I wasn't talking about you." She couldn't help ribbing him. She felt light and joyful, as if everything had changed. "It's surprising how everything has changed, though tonight was like it used to be. But better."

"True. The branding iron booth and the hand-braided harness booths make a real nice addition to the festival." A curve tugged at the corner of his mouth, a sure sign that he knew what she was too shy to speak of.

Was he going to make her say it?

"I wasn't talking about the street vendors." Surely he knew that. Her face heated, the skin tightening as she blushed. She looked away so he wouldn't see it.

"I know." His assurance rumbled comfortingly and he sidled Scout closer. His much larger hand covered hers where it rested on the pommel, and she closed her eyes. Caring ribboned through her, and she twined her fingers between his.

Just like they used to do, they rode toward home through the heavenly path of low slanting light, side by side and hand in hand.

* * *

Her grandparents' house rose into sight when Copper turned into the graveled driveway. Their ride was almost at an end. She pushed aside a knot of disappointment because she wanted the moment to last forever. Did he feel this, too? she wondered. How on earth had she ever been able to hold back her love for him? It whispered through her like the quietest of hymns, somber and reverent and life-affirming. Everything she'd accomplished, every decision she'd made, every day she'd lived had been in an effort to forget him, and it had failed. Through the years, her affection had remained, changed and now renewed. Justin had grown into the man she'd always known he would be, and she loved him more.

Please, she prayed. *Lord, don't let this moment end.*

As if Justin felt the same way, his hand remained clasped in hers, swinging slightly between them as he slowed his horse to an even slower walk. She did the same. Seconds ticked by, but they could delay having to part ways for the night.

"I don't suppose you have plans for Saturday?" His question stirred seeds of hope.

"The rodeo is on Saturday."

"Yes, it is." Dimples cut deep as his grin widened, whole and carefree. "Would you like to go with me?"

"I'd love to." She felt breathless, like a schoolgirl again, dizzy because handsome Justin Granger was asking her out. "But can you leave the ranch unattended?"

"Scotty will keep an eye on things. I figure Dad won't be away for long." His hand tightened around hers, just enough that it felt as if he didn't want to let go.

Please want me the way I want you, she wished. She

wasn't prepared to feel this way. She didn't know if she wanted to trust any man, even Justin again, but her feelings for him were impossible to deny.

"There's still no word on the missing cattle." He changed the subject smoothly.

"It's got to be hard worrying about their welfare," she answered. "Buttercup keeps bawling for her friends. She nearly drove me nuts when I was baking this afternoon. I kept having to come outside and bribe her with molasses treats."

"Which only makes her bawl more often," he pointed out, chuckling.

"Right, well, then I'm really hoping the sheriff finds the cows. That's the best solution."

"Todd isn't too motivated to find three heifers. He didn't bother much with the evidence they left behind."

"Gramps says he put in a complaint to the town council."

"He's not the only one. A lot of ranchers aren't happy with this guy. The Greens on the other side of Mustang Lane were hit by rustlers about nine months ago. Professionals, who brought in helicopters and semis, the whole nine yards. Wiped them out." It was easier to talk about the county's problems with the sheriff instead of asking Rori the one question he'd been holding back.

Was she going to stay? He didn't want to admit it, but he suspected he knew the answer. They'd reached the fork in the driveway, where a well-traveled path was worn into the grass from the road to the small barn. Time to let go of her hand. He hated the sensation of her fingers slipping way from his and the empty feeling inside as he turned away from her. He reined in Scout and dismounted. They'd reached the end of the line.

"I had fun tonight." The best evening he'd had in over a decade because he'd spent it with her. He waited while she swung down, her movements graceful and poised. He could spend a lifetime watching her and he would never tire of seeing her adjusting her ball cap and sparkling with quiet happiness.

She was healing, which was what she'd come home to do. Don't open up to her, he thought but his warning had come too late. The strength of his affection for her was like a flash flood striking without warning, crashing down the protective walls he'd built and laying bare his heart.

"I had the best time." Wide-eyed and vulnerable, she laid her hand in the center of his chest. "It's so good to be home and with you."

If only her bottom lip hadn't vibrated as if with uncertainty, as if she were hoping to be kissed. Then maybe he wouldn't have dipped his head and claimed her. A smart man would proceed with caution, but he wasn't thinking. Emotions drove him to fit their lips together in the softest, most reverent kiss.

She held on tight to him, the sweetest woman on earth, and for that one moment in time she was his. Nothing could come between them—not the past or the unknown future. He felt so close to her as he cradled her cheek with his hand, clinging to her, refusing to break their kiss.

Could she feel how much he loved her? How he'd finally learned what true love was? Could she know just from his kiss that his heart had left with her years ago and now she'd brought it back to him? He was whole because of her. If he ended this kiss, the moment would end. The past would matter and the future she was planning without him. It took all his courage to withdraw from her tender kiss.

Please love me, too, he prayed. But the moment was gone and rational thought returned like an icy wind on the summer's evening. The bright sun could not warm him when he gazed into the violet-blue of her eyes. Had he gone too far? He didn't know, and she didn't say anything. She gazed up at him, maybe it was tender, or maybe she had simply been carried away with the moment.

He didn't like being vulnerable. Wanting her was like flinging open the door to his soul and he stood undefended, wanting what she had never been able to give him.

"Maybe that shouldn't have happened." The words were out before he'd thought them through, words hovering in the air between them.

"Oh." She looked down for an instant, the long shadows hiding her expression.

For one tiny hopeful second he imagined she might be trying to hide her disappointment. That she was attempting to find the words to tell him how important their kiss had been. He wanted her to choose the best course not for his sake but for hers. It was up to her to decide if she wanted him or not. He was not going to make the same mistake this time. As hard as it was, he steeled his spine.

Please choose me, he wished and searched her lovely face for the smallest sign she might want him. He found none.

"If that's the way you feel." She tossed him a carefully controlled smile. "We can always attribute that kiss to the power of the past."

Not to the pull of the future, he realized. Disappointment floored him. He didn't hang his head, and he prayed the agony punching through him didn't show. Drowning in it, he did his best to give her a come-what-may nod and tipped his hat to her.

"Guess so," he said, managing to sound as if he wasn't choking, as if the wind and his unspoken dreams hadn't been knocked out of him. "Guess we got carried away."

"Yes." Polished by the glow from the sunset, she seemed luminous. Or perhaps, he realized, he'd never seen as deep inside her before. It was as if they stood together, hearts open and souls revealed. She did not reach out for him.

He was afraid of reaching for her. If he enfolded her in his arms and kissed her again, would she push him away? If he offered her his love, would she refuse him? She'd done it before and he'd survived it, but he carried the scars with him still. Every day without her had been empty, and if he dared to say the words, to give voice to what he wanted most, a life honoring her, it would crush him if she said no.

Surely, she would say no. He had nothing to offer but life on a working ranch, which meant day after day of hard work and commitment to the animals in his care. In his experience, most women didn't choose that kind of life. He wanted her to be happy. He wanted her to follow her bliss. And if that was in Dallas, then he may as well get it over with now before another day went by and he found himself more in love with her.

"Maybe it would be best if we didn't ride together again." He said the words with regret and because they needed to be said. "Since old times keep getting confused with the new."

"Right." She swallowed hard, holding herself very still. Copper nudged her affectionately, nickering low. "That tricky nostalgia keeps getting in the way. That can't be good."

"That's my thinking, too." He sounded distant, as if

he were talking of the weather or of the latest crop report. "It isn't smart for us to confuse what is with what was. That's how people get hurt."

"Sure. Neither of us want that." She blindly felt for Copper's reins, although the gelding was leaning against her and he would follow her without reins if she asked. She needed something to hold on to, something to do with her hands that felt normal and familiar. The earth seemed to be crumbling at her feet, and she had to hold it together long enough to get safely inside the barn. "I have to get Copper cared for. Thanks for the walk down memory lane tonight. I hope you have a good evening."

"Wait. Are you all right?" He held himself like a mountain, tall and unyielding, larger than life, but his question made her pause. He swept off his Stetson, revealing the rugged planes of his face and a poignant question. Unspoken, he waited for her reply.

No, I'm not in love with you, she wished she were able to tell him. But it wouldn't be the truth. She longed for the shelter of his arms and the light of his love. But she feared he did not feel the same. "I'm fine."

"Oh. Well, good." The question vanished and he looked uncertain for a moment.

Had he wanted a different answer? If she had gathered up her courage to risk her heart, would it have changed things? Or would he still be turning away from her?

Please love me, she wished. If she could have one prayer answered and only one, that's what she would ask for. But true love took two, it was not a one-way street, and so she watched as Justin donned his hat, swung into his saddle and reined Scout away from her.

"Good night." He tipped the brim of his hat, a Western man to the core, looking like everything a woman could ever dream of. He was strength and integrity and what a man ought to be.

"Good night," she managed to say without a single hitch to betray the sorrow building within. She was thankful he wasted no time in disappearing from her sight, galloping down the drive until the shadows stole him. Only then, when he was far enough away not to hear, did she let her heart bleed.

Chapter Fifteen

The fire of sunset lingered long after the sun went down. Atop the ridge overlooking home and stables, Justin spun Lightning in a slow circle, surveying the rise and fall of Granger land stretching beyond sight. After leaving Rori behind, he'd stopped long enough at the house to grab a thermos of coffee. He had to caffeine up for first watch, then he'd rubbed Scout down and settled him in his box stall with a good meal. He'd left the old gelding, then assured a tired-looking Max that he'd worked hard enough on the day shift and chosen one of the quarter horses Dad and Autumn had trained.

The radio strapped to his saddle squawked. Cell coverage in the north hills was patchy, so that meant it was Scotty calling in. Sure enough, the familiar voice crackled to life. "All's quiet here. Do you want me to send Louis to you?"

"No." Justin palmed the handheld. He couldn't keep his mind on his work. "Go ahead and send him home for the rest of the night."

"Roger." The radio squawked out.

In silence again, Justin stowed the radio and searched the dark stretch of land for Cheyenne. He lifted his binoculars for a better look. He'd spotted her horse. She was riding Dreamer tonight and his saddle was empty. It wasn't hard to figure out where she'd gone. He scoped the nearby herd and found her rubbing the bull's poll. The big animal had his forehead down so she could reach it and his eyes closed, looking as if he'd found heaven.

No doubt about it. Cheyenne had Dad's gift with cows. It was their joke that the Grangers were a family of cow whisperers. The Hereford pressed his huge face against Cheyenne's middle, nearly obscuring her from sight. Appearing content, she wrapped her arms around his enormous neck.

If there were any danger around, the bull wouldn't be calm. Justin dropped his binocs and pressed Lightning into a quick walk, heading the length of the ridge. There was another herd to check on before he felt right about taking a coffee break. But as hard as he tried, work didn't keep his thoughts from Rori. They followed him like shadows in the night.

I was right, he told himself as he sat back in the saddle, balancing his weight as Lightning began to pick her way down the steep side of the ridge. He'd been smart to end things. He couldn't go through that again. The bleak grief when he'd lost her had smashed his entire world. He'd never been whole again, his life never right. Something had always been missing and now he knew. She was more than his heart. She always had been and would always be. His devotion to her was absolute.

But she wanted different things. And just as she'd said, when the differences between two people were so great they couldn't be compromised on, heartache was the end result. He remembered his mom and her misery. She'd resented Dad's long hours in the fields and barns. She'd grown bitter at the animals always needing care and attention. She'd felt trapped on the ranch because vacations were nearly nonexistent. The closest mall was a two-hour drive one way. There was no luxurious day spa nearby, just the Glam-A-Rama beauty parlor next to the feed store.

Rori was a country girl, sure, but she'd thrived in a city. She had taught music at a private arts school. There was nothing like that around here. She'd admitted wanting to live in the country maybe on a few acres outside Dallas, but that wasn't the same as living on a remote working ranch. The few options in Wild Horse and on this ranch would limit her. Would she be happy with that?

This evening, she'd been amazing, dazzling him every moment they'd been together. The images of being with her today drove away his doubts and he savored them—the play of the wind in her hair, the notes of her laughter, the harmony of walking at her side. They'd discussed this and that—items in a booth, the funny antics of a kid nearby in the crowd, just small stuff as they bantered back and forth. Happiness filled him as he remembered how she'd captivated him. Her presence was like the first ray of light at the day's beginning and the last gleam at day's end. He was in the dark without her.

He lifted his face to the heavens where stars were blinking to life, one by one, precious light in a universe of darkness. The Lord was out there somewhere in the vast night, a caring God to guide him. But where was he going? He wanted to keep his heart closed, his vulnerable self protected because all signs led to Rori leaving in a few months. Leaving. He did his best not to feel the pain. He adjusted his balance as Lightning skidded the last few steep steps to the grassy floor below, and the meadow lay out ahead of them.

Lord, I don't think You are guiding me to her and it's tearing me apart. He searched the stars, prayer lifting through him. *Dad needs me here. I'm sure this ranch is where You mean me to be. Wherever You are leading Rori, please let it be to somewhere good.*

Dressed for work, Rori tucked her iPod into her pocket and closed her bedroom door behind her. She fumbled her way down the creaking stairs in the dark, drawn by the faint ray of light at the bottom of the stairwell. Kitchen sounds grew louder as she skirted the old upright piano in the living room. Her fingers itched to sit down and play as she'd done last night until bedtime, but two hours of music hadn't chased away her devastation. There was nothing to be done but to hide her heartbreak and face the day.

"Good morning, Pumpkin." Gram turned from the stove, spatula in hand. "Did you get enough sleep?"

"Enough to get by on." She made a beeline straight to the coffeepot, filled a cup and took a sip. In a few seconds the caffeine would kick in; until then she only had to try to seem awake. She saw no need to mention she'd had a hard time settling down last night. Her brain kept going over what Justin had said and what he hadn't.

"It was a pleasure to listen to you play last night." Gram gave the sausages a turn. "You know how I love Beethoven, but I worried about you. You didn't get any wind-down time. I worried you wouldn't be able to get right to sleep. And look at you this morning, all groggy."

"I'll be fine." Hot coffee burned down her throat. "I just wanted to get in some practice. I've been falling down on the job lately."

"I'll say. You haven't touched the piano since you've been here." Gram scooped an omelet from the fry pan, wrapped it around a sausage and packaged it neatly in a paper towel. "Here's your breakfast to go. I ran into Ellen Gibbs at Frontier Days yesterday and do you know what she asked me?"

"I have no idea." Rori kissed her grandmother's cheek and took the breakfast wrap in hand.

"She wanted to know if you would consider giving her granddaughters piano lessons. You know Mrs. Simpson retired last year, and there's no one around to take her students."

Rori recognized the sweet meddlesome look on Gram's face. She hesitated at the door, one hand on the knob. "Are you asking me to stay and teach piano?"

"I'm not the one asking. I'm mentioning it, is all. I told Ellen you already had a job in that fancy music school in Dallas, but she didn't want to listen." Gram grabbed a paper-towel-lined plate and plucked sausage after sausage from the pan. "You have a good day at the Grangers', dear. I suspect you'll see Justin?"

"It would be hard to miss seeing him." Oh, she knew good and well what Gram was getting at. And pointing out the alternative life she could have here instead of returning to Dallas come September wasn't going to change her mind. It wasn't Dallas she was fond of, but she loved teaching and she liked having the assurance of her teaching job waiting for her now that her divorce was all but final.

And it wasn't as if she had a reason to stay. Not if Justin was going to kiss her and then call it a mistake.

Wrestling down heartbreak, she crossed the porch, tripped down the steps and followed the path to the barn. Copper's head came up from grazing, his ears swiveled forward and he nickered a cheerful greeting.

"Hi, handsome!" she called and he came running up to the fence. He lipped her forehead in affection and then tried to steal her omelet. Good thing she was too quick for him. Laughing, she climbed between the fence boards.

You don't get mornings like this in the city. She breathed in the fresh air rising from the growing grass, scented by the apples in the trees nearby. Life here was good. She'd missed the wide-open feeling, of having Copper walking at her side, of never hurrying, and she loved the commute. She grabbed Copper's bridle.

Fine, she could be honest with herself. She'd missed this way of life. It was part of who she was and would always be. And if an inner voice whispered that she would be happy here, that she had a good paying job cooking for the Grangers, then she tried to deny it.

No, it would never work, she thought. Justin would be there and *then* how could she try to drive away the memory of his kiss?

"Hey, Pumpkin." Gramps ambled into sight toting a small pail. "I was just on my way to feed the hens. You look a sight this morning. Didn't you get much sleep?"

"I'm fine, Gramps." Really. It wasn't as if he could mend what was broken. This wasn't a skate or a saddle needing repair, but her heart. "I've just got a lot on my mind."

"Sure. Sending those divorce papers off yesterday had to be wearing on ya." He hesitated, as if he had something he wanted to say but wasn't sure if he should. He tipped back his hat like a cowboy of old, one of the good guys. "Bein' out with that Granger boy had to make things a bit better for you, I suspect."

"Oh, nothing is easy when it comes to Justin Granger."

"That's spoken like a gal in love. I can tell. I've known you since you were yay big." He held up his hands, two feet apart, the small bucket swinging. "I don't suppose it's your feelings that are the problem, but his?"

"I lost my chance with him long ago." She set down her cup, laid her breakfast wrap on top of it, and gently eased the bit into Copper's mouth.

"What are you talkin' about?" Gramps shook his head as if in disbelief, scattering fine gray hairs. He gave his overalls a hitch. "That boy's never fallen out of love with you. Everyone in these parts knows it. Why can't you see it?"

"Because that's just wishful thinking on your part, and I won't be tempted into believing you're right." She tossed him a smile as Copper tried stealing her breakfast again. "Besides, I'm going back to Dallas in two months."

"Is that what you want?"

"Sure. Why wouldn't it be?" She would have earned enough money working for the Grangers to buy a used car and to put down a deposit and first month's rent on an apartment. She would be back on her feet and back to her life.

Except it had began to feel as if her life was right here.

Gramps tilted his head, listening. "That's your grandmother calling me. Guess I'd better go see what bee she's got in her bonnet."

She smoothed a saddle blanket across Copper's withers, carefully making sure there wasn't a single wrinkle before she shouldered the saddle in place. As she worked, her grandparents' conversation drifted faintly through the open barn doors.

"Hey! Who's that good-looking woman standing on my back porch?" Gramps whistled.

"The woman who has your breakfast ready and waiting, you sweet talker."

"I'm glad you think so. Want me to whisper sweet nothings in your ear?"

"You've been dragging your feet this morning and now I'm waiting on you. What I want is for you to put down that pail. You can feed the chickens later. Get in here before the eggs get cold. And, no, a kiss isn't going to charm me."

"Then how about two?"

Copper stomped his foot, eager to be off, as she tightened the cinch and lowered the stirrups. Rori led him out of the barn just in time to see Gramps taking Gram's hand. He lit up with adoration as he helped his beloved up the porch steps, his devotion to her strong and flawless.

They made love look so easy. She watched with a touch of wistfulness as the couple bowed their heads together in soft conversation. Whatever Gramps said made Gram brighten like dawn. Happiness wreathed her lovely face as she passed through the screen door he held open for her and they both disappeared from sight.

Could love like that ever be possible for her? She swung into the saddle, juggling her coffee and breakfast, and reined Copper toward Granger land. Justin was the only man she wanted to love with all her might for the rest of her life. No other man, not even the one she'd loved enough to marry, had even come close.

She felt infinitely alone as she rode into the peaceful fields accompanied by lark song, alone and with some decisions to make.

* * *

Justin stumbled down the stairs, fighting grogginess and a headache from lack of sleep. This afternoon he was interviewing a half dozen applicants, but until he hired a few extra hands he would be pulling double shifts. Although their herd was insured and losing them would be a hard blow to the ranch, he was more concerned about the animals. Men ruthless enough to steal weren't usually the sort who put the care and needs of cows ahead of their own. That was the reason for the tension headache, but not his sleeplessness.

After he'd checked on the expecting mare, given Dad and Autumn a report and stumbled to bed, he hadn't been able to turn off his brain. He'd kept thinking of Rori, going over and over their kiss. It had felt right, as if it were meant to be. The way she held on to him, the way she kissed him back with all the innocence she possessed.

But it hadn't been right. Going over and over the moment stirred up regrets and wishes that tore at him. He should have known better than to have let down his guard. What were the chances she would leave? That she wouldn't choose him? He should have kept his distance, never relented on his decision to keep far away from her.

He pounded into the kitchen and the scent of brewing coffee was a clue. Too late to put on the brakes and find another way out of the house. Rori and Autumn looked up, caught in the middle of a conversation. He tore his gaze away but not before he noticed Rori's paleness and the dark circles beneath her eyes. Hadn't she slept much, either?

"I was telling Rori about Paullina," Autumn explained as she popped the last bite of a muffin into her mouth. "It could be any minute now, so she needs to be watched."

"I can do it," he clipped out, fully aware the woman in question had turned her back and was breaking eggs into a fry pan at the stove.

Pain rolled through him. He didn't know what he expected. He'd been the one to tell her he didn't mean that kiss—a lie if there ever was one. He was not a lying man, and he hadn't thought of it as one at the time. But a lie it was because he'd meant that kiss, he was no longer sorry about it. If he thought it would change the courses of their future, then he would haul her into his arms and kiss her as much as it took for her to stay.

But he wouldn't because he wanted what was best for her. He wanted her to be happy. She'd chosen a life away from him and small-town life once. No, he had to be practical. Why would she want anything different this time around?

"Good," he ground out to Autumn's explanation and pounded straight to the mudroom, bypassing the pot of coffee. His head pounded worse at the thought of a morning without it, but he didn't want to get any closer to Rori than he had to. It hurt too much.

He jammed his right foot into his left boot. Great. He sat on the bench, yanked it off and grabbed the right boot. A movement in the doorway had to be her. He'd know her willowy grace anywhere. He kept his gaze on his laces as he tied a quick knot.

"I thought you might need this." The soft melody of her voice rippled through him, beauty he did not want to feel. There was a scrape as she set the travel mug on the bench beside him and the air crackled from her nearness. He breathed in the scent of roses and lost dreams as she moved away.

Don't look at her, he thought. Maybe that would keep him from hurting. He willed steel into his chest.

"Thanks," he grumbled. Knowing full well she'd paused in the archway between the rooms and stood waiting for a better response from him, he grabbed the left boot, jammed his foot into it and fumbled with the laces. He hated that show of weakness, the proof of how much she meant to him. He grabbed the cup, hopped to his feet and pounded out the door.

"Justin?"

One word from her stopped him. He froze in the threshold. Don't turn around, he ordered even as everything within him wanted to face her and to savor every moment with her for as long as he could.

She isn't going to stay, cowboy, he told himself and kept going. "I'll be out in the fields, but close enough for you to call if any trouble comes up."

"I, uh—" She'd obviously wanted to say something else, but changed her mind. "Okay. I'll keep a breakfast plate in the oven in case you need it."

"I won't," he said flatly, marching across the back porch. He'd eat the months-old energy bars in his saddlebag before he'd let hunger drive him into the kitchen alone with her. He was trying to be smart, in control, to follow the path God had laid before him.

But it didn't make him happy as he felt her pain. Regardless of how much distance grew between them that hurt remained, an unbearable connection he could not break.

Buttercup bleated, front feet braced, putting all her might into her plaintive moo. Her chocolate eyes implored him to come keep her company and to let her check out his shiny metallic cup.

"Sorry, sweetheart," he told her, striding on by, fighting with himself to keep from turning around to catch a glimpse of Rori one more time. He had to keep on going. It was the only smart choice.

Stop thinking about him, she told herself as she wiped down the counter and hit the start button that set the dishwasher to gurgling and whooshing. The big, pleasant kitchen echoed around her. Everyone had rotated in on shifts to eat and had gone back to their work, except for Justin and a few of the hired men who left for home and a bit of sleep.

It was grocery day. She'd penned a long list. Running around-the-clock shifts, Frank had asked her to make hearty meals to keep everyone alert and full of energy. She planned on making granola and homemade trail mix, perfect for snacks that packed well in saddlebags, and was debating on whether to make brownies or chocolate-chip cookies when the screen door made a strange sound.

Curious, she put down her pen and peered around the edge of the island. Buttercup stood on the porch, her rope tangled on the boards. The cow, caught in the act of mouthing the door handle, stopped and flashed her innocent eyes. A puppy couldn't have looked sweeter.

"What do you think you're doing?" She abandoned her list and crossed the room. "You've pulled up your picket stake. Don't tell me you're trying to open the door."

As if to say, Okay, I won't, Buttercup fluttered her long curly lashes and tried not to look guilty.

"You're awful pleased with yourself." She turned the handle, as Buttercup grinned with delight and watched the door open a few inches with wonder.

"You're not coming in, pretty girl. Excuse me, out of the way. Let's get you—"

Buttercup interrupted with a loud moo, glanced over her shoulder toward the horse pasture and mooed again. Rori noticed that Paullina, the mare she'd been checking on throughout the morning, wasn't in sight.

"Funny, she was there a few minutes ago. Back up, Buttercup." Since the cow had a mind of her own, Rori managed to wedge her arm through the crack between the screen door and the jamb and push on the cow's sturdy shoulder. Grudgingly, the animal stepped back enough to allow Rori to slip through. She grabbed Buttercup's halter. She didn't like the twist of worry in her stomach. Something felt wrong. "C'mon, girl. Let's go check on Paullina."

As if in agreement, Buttercup mooed, awkwardly turned around in the relatively small space and clomped down the steps as if she were no stranger to them. Rori didn't even want to know how many times previously Buttercup had tried to let herself into the house.

She led the cow across the front lawn, no sense wasting time fussing with the stake, and tried to calm the quivery feeling shaking her knees. Where was the mare? All she saw was lush green grass and the otherwise empty field.

"You were a good girl to come get me," she told Buttercup, tying her quickly to one of the fence posts. Buttercup nodded as if she were already aware of that fact and watched as Rori climbed through the fence boards.

"Paullina?" she called gently. "Are you all right?"

Insects buzzed lazily around her in the midmorning air and a killdeer squeaked, startled, as Rori crunched through the soft, crackly grass. The bird cried out and tucked her wing at a strange angle. Feigning a broken wing, she ran away from a hidden nest. Rori ignored her and kept going.

"Paullina?" She called, her voice echoing back to her. "Where's the good, pretty girl?"

No answer. She found the mare down in a hollow of grass, lather flecking her beautiful white coat and groaning in pain. Rori dug her phone from her pocket and dialed Justin's number without thought, her heart reaching out to him. She knew it always would.

Chapter Sixteen

The wide-open spaces felt good, just what he'd been needing to chase away the lingering effects of Rori's presence. Sorrow had lodged deep in his chest, whether it was hers or his he could no longer tell.

Justin reined Max to a halt along the fence line and dismounted to check on the newly branded calves. He knew Cheyenne and Addison would be along later to check the little ones for any signs of infection or discomfort, but he needed to walk a bit to clear his head. Somehow he had to find a solution to Rori and how much he wanted to love her.

"Hey, Clancy," he crooned to the bull. At the sound of his name the big Hereford ambled over, head up and proud to be in charge of his herd. "Everything all right?"

The bull lowed, a comforting sound deep in his throat, and offered his poll for rubbing. Justin obliged, and the satisfaction of being where he belonged rolled through him.

Could he leave this place? he wondered. His dad wanted to retire in a few more years, and the ranch had grown by thousands of acres over the time he'd helped to manage it. So had the number of cow/calf pairs ranging it. The ranch had grown to be too much for one person to run alone, if he left Autumn to do the job.

Family had always come first, but which family did he choose—the one he'd grown up with or the one he wanted to find? He tried to consider his life elsewhere. Not that he was going anywhere, but it didn't hurt to wonder what if. Selling out his share of the herd would make him very comfortable. He could go where he wanted and do what he wanted.

He could be with Rori.

Lord, surely this isn't You putting doubts in my head. Justin felt a tug on his jeans leg. He looked down to find two cows grabbing a hold of him, teeth locked on the denim hem.

"Did you ladies want some attention, too?" Apparently they did because they tugged harder. He didn't have time to lift his free hand to oblige them with a pat and a stroke. Other cows came up from behind him, affectionately lipping his shirt, licking his boots, stealing his hat.

Okay, maybe that was answer enough. He was happy here, and considering leaving a life he loved on the hope that Rori's feelings for him had changed was a fool's course. As much as he wanted her, the memory of being twenty-one and proposing to the love of his life returned, the one obstacle he could not defeat. When she'd whispered no, she could not, it had been the end of his world. A man couldn't take that kind of a blow a second time no matter how much he wanted to.

Or could he? Was it worth the risk?

An electronic chime sounded from his jeans. One of the cows, curious about the noise, attacked his pocket. He snatched back his hat, thumbed out his phone and frowned at the screen. Rori. His thumb hit the answer button before he could think about it. "What's wrong?"

"It's Paullina." Panic snapped in her voice, an urgency he'd never heard before. "She's down. I've checked her and I think everything is all right, but please come. I don't want to do this by myself."

"You won't be alone as long as I'm near." Every fiber of his being responded. Instant tension telegraphed through him as he extricated the hem of his T-shirt from one cow and his untied bootlace from another. He raced straight for Max. "Keep her calm. This isn't her first foal, so she knows what's going on."

"Should I call the vet?"

"I've got Nate on speed dial." He swung into the saddle and wheeled Max toward home. As if the gelding understood, he broke into a hard gallop. The ground flew by in a blur. "Hang tight and I'll give him a call."

"Thanks, Justin." She sighed, a rush of relief that told him she'd been worried he might have refused to help.

Didn't she know he wasn't made that way? She ought to know him better than that. He wondered exactly what circumstances had changed her back in Dallas. Lord help him, but he had to fight to keep the sympathy from his voice. "No worries. I'm four minutes away."

Maybe this was God's answer, he pondered, as he and Max raced home.

"That's it, Paullina." Rori stroked her fingertips across the horse's neck. She sat in the sun-warmed grass next to the mare, doing her best to keep the animal comforted. She'd never found herself alone with a foaling mare before. Assisting wasn't the same as helping, she realized, glancing toward the corral where Wildflower grazed with the sprightly filly Cheyenne had named Rosebud.

"You're going great," she reassured her. The horse's head came up and she stroked her cheek, gently calming her. "Just lie back. You are such a good girl."

Paullina nickered low in her throat, as if she were grateful for the company. Her sides heaved, and she thrashed a little in pain. Four minutes away, Justin had promised. She checked her watch. Only three minutes had ticked past. It felt as if a century had gone by.

Maybe because she was dreading being alone with him. She couldn't forget the way he'd been this morning, hardly looking at her. His painful aloofness puzzled her. How could he have kissed her so perfectly with endless affection, and where had that affection gone? Last night, just when she'd been ready to believe again, just when she could see a glimpse of his tenderness, he'd turned away. He'd called it a mistake.

Would he ever be able to open up to her?

Hoof beats echoed across the long expanse of sloping hillside and verdant fields. She whipped around. Justin rode with the sun at his back, wide shoulders braced and invincible. Her most cherished dream.

Max approached the fence and Justin dismounted while the horse was still moving. Buttercup bellowed to him, as if to explain the circumstances. Was that a smile cracking the stony line of his chiseled mouth? He patted the cow's neck, ducked between the fencing and strode her way.

Remember to breathe, she told herself. Somehow she had to keep her feelings firmly reined in. But as his long-legged stride brought him closer, her pulse skipped beats. Her palms went damp. Last night's kiss tingled across her lips.

You can do this. She lifted her chin and hoped she looked dignified. "She's progressing fast."

"I got a hold of Dad and Autumn, too. We'll see who gets here first, the foal or everyone I called." Nothing rattled Justin. He was solid and steady as the earth beneath her, a Western hero of old striding in to save the day. He halted where the vulnerable horse could see him and held out a hand to stroke the mare's nose.

"Hey, girl, looks like you're about to become a mama." Low, soft tones as smooth as molasses. He moved in slowly, carefully aware of Paullina's steeled hooves. "I plan on helping you out. Is that okay with you?"

Paullina answered with a part nicker, part groan. Lather flecked her beautiful white coat as she struggled against the pain, caught in the grips of a contraction.

"This won't take long at all." His hand covered hers completely, and Rori startled. The contact struck her like lightning all the way to the soul. Was it her imagination, or was there a hint of affection in his dark blue eyes? Caring in his sun-warmed touch?

Her heart swooped right up in adoration, knowing it was true.

"Are you doing okay?" he asked.

"I'm fine. Do you need me to get anything?"

"We should be fine for now. I want to make sure we've got both hooves pointing in the right direction. You keep doing what you're doing." The connection between them remained even after his hand lifted from hers and he moved away, talking softly to the mare.

For the first time in a long time she didn't second-guess her choices or feel the need to examine the decisions she'd made in her life. The regret and fears of mistakes vanished, leaving only Justin kneeling nearby. The warm sun beat on her shoulders, the pleasant wind whispered through the grass. Dandelions and daisies fluttered nearby and Paullina groaned, straining against her pain.

She couldn't see what was going on as she stroked the mare's neck in reassurance, but she had a perfect view of Justin helping to deliver the foal. Straightening front hooves, helping to pull with each contraction, cleaning the little nose when it appeared.

"Welcome, little one." Justin's deep tone rumbled through her like homecoming. He was stroking the tiny creature, who lay panting in the grass glistening and miraculous. Infinitely gentle, the big man reassured the newborn, who gazed up at him as if he were an amazing sight.

Truly amazing, Rori decided, giving Paullina one last stroke of comfort before easing onto her feet. She moved slowly as she didn't want to startle the baby. Nothing could be cuter. She twisted up inside with love for the foal, a precious bundle of new life, all long legs and big brown eyes.

"She's as pretty as her mama." He chuckled when the filly shook her head, ruffling her bristled mop of mane and blinked her lashes, as if she couldn't believe her eyes. Apparently she was very surprised to see a second human.

"She's adorable." Rori eased down in the grass on one knee next to Justin. It felt like a century ago when she and Justin had admired Wildflower's foal and the pain of the past had been an unbreachable wall between them. Where had it gone?

She did not know. Somehow it had vanished. Justin's unguarded gaze found hers. She felt the impact like a hook to her soul and she was caught, bonded to him for all eternity. Only this moment mattered and the unspoken comfort of a love that nothing could diminish.

He felt it, too—she knew he did—for he reached across a cluster of daisies and cradled her hand in his. The hook deepened in her soul, binding them with a strength only grace could do.

"Rori, I—" That was as far as he got. Paullina whinnied, recognizing Frank, who was striding through the field, his horse Rogue lathered and waiting alongside Buttercup and Justin's Max.

"Looks like I missed the big event." Frank bounded up to check on Paullina. The mare struggled to her feet and with a quiet nicker, put her head in Frank's hands. "That's one fine baby you've got, sweetheart."

Justin released her, and Rori felt awkward sitting there. Autumn was riding into sight, and the rumble of an approaching engine told her the vet was moments away. No sense sitting around instead of lending a hand. She rose, aware of Justin's silence as she backed away. There was no distance far enough nor any defense strong enough to hold back her love for him.

The men stood by as Paullina licked her baby affectionately. The precious filly rested fawnlike in the grass, watching her new world with fascination and taking it all in. At the sidelines, Buttercup bellowed as if to announce the birth to the entire ranch.

Larks sang and a hummingbird hovered above a honeysuckle bloom next to the porch step as she skipped by. When she glanced over her shoulder, Justin was watching. Maybe it was the distance or maybe it was wishful thinking, but she saw love on his face, the sort of love a woman dreamed of finding, a once-in-a-lifetime gift.

* * *

"There you go, girl." Justin dumped the measure of grain into the feed trough in the comfortable box stall. Paullina dove in, sweeping up the treat, leaning her shoulder against him in affection. He patted her velvety neck before moving away. Rori kept returning to his thoughts like a favorite song playing over and over.

"Looks like you've got a lot on your mind, son." Frank held open the gate, looking serious. "You okay?"

Not much got past his father, Justin had to give him credit for that.

"Fair to middling." He waited for Frank to latch the gate, watching the little foal, as perfectly white as her mother. Addison had named her Snowflake. "I'd better get back to work."

"Come with me." Frank inclined his head toward the door, a single nod, but his gaze was grim. "Just got off the phone with the state patrol. Seems a truck and trailer broke down on the interstate near the Montana line. They found our girls inside."

"The cows?" Dad didn't look happy, so something was wrong. Justin passed a hand over his face, preparing for bad news. "Are they okay?"

"Starved, dehydrated, beaten and Jasmine is down. She couldn't get up. Don't know why yet, but the patrolman said they had a vet on the way. It's possible they are going to need my authorization to euthanize."

"Ah, Dad, I'm sorry." He was sorry for the animal and for his father who had bottle-raised the cow. "I'll hitch the trailer and we can be on the road in ten minutes, tops."

"I've already sent Addison to the house to pack for us. It'll be an overnight trip, so we'll need enough feed in the trailer. I'll see to that."

"What about Rori?" He glanced toward the house, where large windows winked in the noontime sun.

"She's in town grocery shopping."

"Oh." He hadn't noticed her leaving because he'd been getting the stall comfortable and cozy for the new mama and her baby. The strong sunshine burned his eyes as he broke away from his dad. Buttercup was now in the brood mare's empty meadow, drowsing after an exciting morning.

He wanted to talk to Rori before he went. He couldn't tell her he loved her, that he wanted to spend his life with her because nothing had changed, well, nothing between them. When he'd thundered into the yard on Max and spotted her sitting with the horse, love had hit him so hard he could not breathe. Every step he took toward her had doubled it. She sat unknowing with the wind tangling her hair and the sunlight blessing her. All that mattered, all that would ever matter, was her.

He hopped into his truck, started the engine, backed out of the garage and up the lane along the lawn, speeding up the stretch to the second stable behind the barn. Dad had opened the bay doors and stood beside the trailer, hands up and gesturing, guiding him in. He kept his father in the side-view mirror, turning a tad to the left, easing up on the gas, hitting the brake, and where was his mind?

On Rori. On how serene she'd looked this morning and her awe making her even more compelling when she saw the new foal for the first time. She understood the wonder of life on this ranch, the miracle of each life, the importance of safeguarding God's creatures and the emotional reward that went with it. For a moment, he'd almost believed she might want to share the journey with him.

Alone in the truck, he tossed his hat on the crew seat behind him. The truck's shocks dipped slightly as his dad made quick work of hitching up. Justin had just enough time to decide to be honest. There was one more thing troubling him, one problem he'd refused to face so far. He would leave this ranch for Rori, and he hoped she would want to stay here. But finding out was a risk that shook him to the marrow. How did a man as closed off as he'd become open his heart? Take a risk, when he'd been playing it safe for so long?

The passenger door swung open and Frank climbed in. "We're hitched and ready to roll." He hit the dash with the flat of his hand. "Let's go, pilot."

"Will do, copilot." Justin put the truck in gear and eased out into the lane, the trailer rattling slightly behind them.

Addison met them near the house with two small duffel bags, an insulated food carrier and two cans of root beer. "I've said like ten prayers for a safe trip and for our cows. You'll call and let us know as soon as you see them?"

"Promise." Justin dropped the bags in the back and handed the carrier and one of the cans over to his dad. After a quick exchange of last-minute ranch concerns and goodbyes, Justin nosed the truck down the driveway.

"You and Rori looked mighty cozy when I rode up." Frank popped his can open and took a slurp. "It's good to see you two together."

"We're not together." He glanced in the rearview. The light dust cloud rising up behind the truck obliterated home from his sight.

"If you two aren't an item, then what are you?"

"I don't want to talk about this, Dad." He turned onto Mustang Lane, heading away from town and away from where Rori was. He imagined her pushing a cart through the only grocery store in town, checking prices, her hair tumbling down from her baseball cap and so precious he would give his life for hers. What if she didn't feel the same way?

"Sure, I get that." Frank took another sip of root beer. "But don't forget life is about risks. God sets a path for us, but if we don't take the first step then we are hurting ourselves and disappointing Him."

"And did I ask for your advice?"

"No, but you're going to get it anyway." He grinned and put his can in the cup holder. "You and that girl are made for each other. Everyone knows it. Don't you think God might be giving you two a second chance? If you don't get this right, Justin, maybe God doesn't have another chance lined up for you. Maybe this is it."

"Fine by me." It wasn't, but he sure wanted it to be. He wanted to be invincible steel so nothing could hurt him again.

"Do you want to end up like me?"

"What's wrong with ending up like you?"

"A lot. Is this my fault? Is that what I've done?" He blew out a breath, holding in the torment that only the truth could bring. "You've been learning by my example."

"Dad, what are you talking about?"

"I've been a widower for nearly sixteen years. Being single is a lonely road and not one I want for you." He may as well be honest. "I don't even want it for myself."

"You said after we lost Mom, never again."

"I did." Truth be told, the marriage had torn him into pieces and he'd needed time to heal up. A lot of time. "Just because things went so wrong with me and your mom, doesn't mean I wouldn't do it all over again."

"What? I was there. I saw how miserable you both were. Mom hated this ranch, at least in the end."

"It didn't start out that way." Bittersweet to remember those years and the risk he'd taken in asking the pretty new girl just moved to town to have a milkshake with him at Clem's. "If I hadn't married Lainie, then I wouldn't have had the privilege of raising the five best kids in the world."

"Rori is going to leave at the end of the summer. It's not the same situation."

"Then I guess what I'm trying to say is this. Life is a demanding trail ride. The pain and the struggle is part of the experience. Sometimes you get knocked to the ground, but what happens if you don't get up? You don't finish the ride, you don't get to your destination. Maybe the reward you find there is worth the pain and the risk." He thought of Cady Winslow, and his own fears of taking the first step on the trail of romance again. "When you get it right, that's the best life has to offer. Love is the greatest thing there is."

"Maybe that's true." His son smiled, actually smiled, and Frank believed that life was going to work out just right for his boy. God would make sure of it.

Chapter Seventeen

Rori wrapped her arms around Copper's neck, holding her best friend close. The old horse nickered warmly, leaning into her, too. She treasured the moment with him, for they did not need words to communicate and drank in the companionable silence. She kissed his warm coat and let go.

"I'll be back with a treat in a bit." She climbed through the fence, already missing him. She'd longed for him every day of every year she'd lived away. She couldn't stomach the thought of doing that again, which was why she'd made a few calls. Why she had liked the idea of becoming a private music teacher.

The grass crackled beneath her shoes as she crossed the back lawn. A robin watched her from a low branch of the apple tree. A hummingbird zipped past her left shoulder on the way to the red feeder swinging from the porch eave. Gramps was nearly through filling a wheelbarrow at the garden's edge, where Gram sat on a low wooden stool, yanking weeds.

"I thought you were supposed to wait for me." She

marched beneath the shade of two ancient plum trees. "What did you promise me when I moved in?"

"That we would let you earn your keep." Gramps winked at her, taking hold of the wheelbarrow's grips and pushing it forward. "Don't look at me. I tried to tell her, but you know women. Don't listen to a thing us poor men have to say." He winked, heading off to the compost pile behind the garage.

"That man." Grams laughed, shaking her head. The bonnet she wore shaded her face and looked dear on her. "He doesn't want you working too hard either. You've put in a long day at the Grangers. I'm used to pulling my own weeds."

"Yes, but I'm here now." She knelt between the rows of lacy green carrot leaves and began plucking at the familiar fronds of a budding dandelion. "You could have at least waited for me."

"Gardening is a pleasure. Feeling the earth between your fingertips, tending God's green growing things, looking forward to the day I can pull these carrots and put them in a salad. It all makes me happy."

"I see that." Gram did have the secret to happiness, that was for sure. Regardless of what life tossed her way, she remained strong and optimistic and sure of her course. "Can I ask you something?"

"That's what I'm here for." Gram set down her trowel, ready to listen.

"When you have two choices in front of you, how do you know which is the right one?" She'd been pondering her decisions all day, but her regrets haunted her. Before she made a move, she had to be sure. "I've prayed on it, I've asked for guidance but I'm not sure of the signs. I've made so many mistakes already in my life. I don't want to make any more."

"What mistakes have you made?" So caring and wise, Gram reached out and covered Rori's hands with hers. "You have done wonderfully, Pumpkin. Your grandfather and I are so proud of you. Besides, what we often call mistakes are really God's way of teaching us what He most wants us to learn."

Tears burned her eyes. "The marriage was a failure, Gram. You know it is. My failure. What if I do it again?"

"God makes no mistakes. The best anyone can do is to trust the Lord and follow your heart. If you do those two things, then you will wind up where you most need to go. And that's never a misstep, dear one." Gram's grip tightened with loving comfort in the perfect evening's light. The approaching sunset cast a golden glow that crowned their piece of Wyoming as if with a promise from heaven.

Follow her heart? Rori swallowed hard, lifted her chin and rubbed at a smear of dirt on her grandmother's cheek. Her choices were suddenly clear.

"There you two are!" A familiar baritone broke through the crowded Wild Horse main street, where the weekend festivities of Frontier Days were in full swing. "Cheyenne told me to keep an eye out for you."

Justin squinted at Tucker, the younger, nearly identical copy of their dad moseying their way. His little brother was dressed in typical Western wear: Stetson, plaid shirt, Levi's and boots. A sight for sore eyes. "Glad you could make it, Tucker."

"My boy." Dad clapped his prodigal son in a one-armed hug and patted his back. "Didn't expect you'd show up."

"I dislocated my shoulder last weekend so the doc ordered me off the circuit for a few weeks." Tucker didn't seem too troubled by it, although his left arm was in a blue sling. "So I figured I might as well drive home for the big shindig. I got in this morning while you were away. Autumn put me to work keeping guard on the north ridge. Did you get the cows put up all right?"

"Yep, and Nate's been to check on them, too," Justin answered. It had been the first thing they'd done when they'd arrived home a few hours ago. "We have Jasmine in the barn recovering."

"Nate thinks she's bruised a few organs but ought to heal up just fine." Frank shrugged, an effort to hide how upset he'd been. "They've been through an ordeal, but they are all right now."

"Already spoiling them, huh?" Tucker winked.

"That's my job," their dad answered with a wink.

Autumn and Addison wandered into sight, colorful snow cones in hand, and they weren't alone.

"Look who we found by the snow cone booth," Autumn announced. "Cady's decided to board with us after all. Isn't that great news?"

Justin was the only one who noticed that their dad went pale.

"Now I have to learn how to ride." The elegant lady blushed, as if that were an embarrassment. "It seems everyone here knows how. I've heard there's nothing to it. But it seems I have a lot to learn before I get onto the back of a horse. That is a long way to fall."

"I'm sure Autumn could teach you what you need to know," their dad spoke up. "Since you'll be coming around to the ranch and all."

"That would be nice." Cady Winslow smiled, blushing a little when her gaze met Frank's.

Well, this is going to be interesting, Justin thought. He caught sight of Rori's golden hair in the crowd, standing with her back to him while her grandfather bought two cones of mint chocolate-chip ice cream. Seeing her made the world, even his family, fade into the background until there was only Rori, his one true love.

"Cady's here all alone," Addison said as if from a great distance. "So we invited her to come sit with us in the stands. We'd better start heading over. Cheyenne's event starts in fifteen minutes."

"You go on ahead without me," he told his family, hardly noticing as they drifted away. He didn't remember crossing the street, only that he was suddenly close enough to hear her conversation.

"No, that's great, I'll take it." She was on her cell, chatting away with a smile in her voice. Her hair, down today, fluttered lightly with her movements, brushing against her back like the finest silk. "First and last month's rent and a security deposit? Sure. I'll write a check and get it to you."

That was the first hit of uncertainty, but he kept on going, his chin up, his spine braced. Hearing his boots on the pavement, she spun around, flipping the phone shut in one hand. She lit up when she saw him. The brilliance of her beauty both inside and out was unbearably bright, and he was no longer standing in shadow.

"Justin, good to see you, young man." Del Cornell handed one mint-green waffle cone to his wife and kept the other. "Heard you found your stolen cows."

"We did, sir. We were lucky the truck hauling them broke down. They were taking them out of state to sell."

"Guess at least those hooligans won't be bothering the cattle around here again." Del nodded, his eyes glinting with understanding. "We'll leave you two young people to talk. I've got a hot date with the prettiest gal in White Horse county."

"Going over to the rodeo isn't a hot date," Rori's grandmother pointed out merrily. "If you want to make this a date, then you better take me out to supper, Del."

"As you wish." The two ambled away, arm in arm, their lifelong love another reason to believe.

"I couldn't help overhearing," he said, jamming his hands into his pockets so he didn't reach for her. He yearned to draw her into the shelter of his arms and hold her there, to never let her go. "Sounded like you found a place to live."

"Yes, I did." She slipped her phone into her back pocket, adorable in a pretty summer top and matching shorts. Her flip-flops kept rhythm as they turned in unison and headed slowly down the street. "I've found a place where I can take Copper with me."

"He'll like that." His palms had broken out in a sweat and a knot of doom had formed and taken over his stomach, but he knew the Lord had brought him here for a reason. Dad was right, this was his second chance. He could open up and show her how he felt. He could be vulnerable. It was the only way to have a happily-ever-after with Rori. He took a deep breath, gathered his courage and opened his heart. "Don't move to Dallas."

"Dallas?" She stopped, turning toward him, an adorable crinkle of surprise marring her forehead.

"At least not without me." He seized the opportunity and got down on one knee, fumbling in his shirt pocket for the ring he'd dug out of the safe back at home. He took hold of her left hand. "You are the love of my life, Rori Cornell. I will move to Texas if that's what you want. Or we can stay here and build a house, say on the quarter section next to your grandparents' property. All I care about is you. Marry me. Please don't leave me again."

"I wasn't going anywhere." Her hand in his trembled. "I rented a little house on the edge of town. I've decided to stay in Wild Horse."

"You have?" That was news to him. She'd decided to stay, but she hadn't given him a yes or no answer.

"My grandparents are getting older and they need a little help around the place. With the garden. Helping with the housework. That kind of thing." Her fingers curled through his, holding on so tight.

"That's good." This is where she rejects me, he thought, waiting for the blow of pain. She hadn't said yes to him. His love for her was so strong, surely it was not a one-way street? "No wonder Del and Polly looked so happy. They're glad you will be nearby."

"Yes." She bit her bottom lip nervously, her violet-blue gaze so intense she could see his soul. "Yes, Justin."

"Yes?" It didn't sink in at first. It took him a few beats before realization hit him. She had agreed to marry him. She wanted to be his wife.

His wife. Joy burst through him, stronger because his heart was open, his walls were down. Happiness filled every piece of him. Every dream he'd ever had burst to life—dreams of her, of their wedding day, the birth of their first child. Hopeful images of years to come paraded across his soul. They could do this, he thought. They could be happily-ever-after.

"I was prepared for this to go the other way," he confessed.

"Why would I say no to you?" Her voice softened, layered with all of her love revealed. "Long ago I asked you to wait, and you did. You let me come back to you."

"I never stopped loving you." Apparently it was a day for confessions. Now that he'd started, he couldn't seem to stop.

"I didn't either." She stared at the ring he slipped rather shakily onto the fourth finger of her left hand. "That's a beautiful diamond."

"It was my grandmother's." His gaze searched hers with one single question. "She and my grandfather had a long and happy life together."

"That's what I want with you." Like the sun's heat against her cheek, she could feel the assurance from heaven. This was their chance to get it right. She intended to do just that and give him her whole heart without reservations. "I love you, Justin Granger."

"I love you more." The truth of it rang in his voice and in the chambers of her heart. He rose to his full height, towering over her, tenderness transforming him. "I promise that I will never stop loving you. Everything I am and everything I have is yours forever."

He took her into his arms, oblivious of the crowd around them buying waffle cones and sun catchers and weather vanes. Kids ran and shouted while parents watched, couples held hands and the mayor called out a hello to the minister. With the sounds of life surrounding them, Justin's arms enfolded her gently against his chest. She closed her eyes, snuggled her cheek against his cotton shirt, joy spiraling through her. She felt full up and brimming over with gratitude.

Thank You, Lord, she prayed. All of her trials and life lessons had led her back to Justin, to the love of her life.

She knew exactly how precious he was, this good man who would not falter, who was the other half of her soul.

"Break it up!" the mayor commented with good cheer as he strolled by. "Justin, isn't your sister competing soon?"

"Pretty soon," he agreed.

"Then get a move on to the stands!" Whistling, Tim Wisener went on his way, calling out to others, reminding them of the barrel race about to take place.

"I guess we should go watch Cheyenne compete," she said, loath to let go of him.

"We should," he agreed, but he didn't move either. "There's one thing I'd like to do first."

"Which is?"

"Kiss my fiancée."

"This is my favorite part," she quipped.

His smile became a kiss, flawless and sweet, his unspoken promise of their happiness to come—enough happiness to see them through a lifetime. She wrapped her arms around his neck and held on tight.

* * * * *

*Don't miss Jillian Hart's next
inspirational romance,
PATCHWORK BRIDE,
available from Love Inspired Historicals,
August 2010.*

Dear Reader,

Welcome to my new family, The Grangers. I hope you can sit down, get comfortable, put up your feet and set your worries aside for a few hours and let the story of Rori Cornell and Justin Granger carry you away to a very special place. Stowaway Ranch is the Granger family's Wyoming ranch, which has been in their family for generations. I also grew up on an original family homestead, where I spent my days caring for cattle and enjoying the beauty of God's countryside. I've hidden several memories from my own childhood on these pages—kamikaze hummingbirds, deer grazing in the fields and a terribly spoiled pet cow are just some of them. Writing the Grangers' stories is like coming home for me, and I hope you feel the same. I also hope you enjoy falling in love along with Justin and Rori as they try to listen to the Lord and figure out where He is leading them.

Autumn's book is next and so is another installment of Frank and Cady's budding romance. HIS HOLIDAY BRIDE will be released in October.

Thank you for choosing THE RANCHER'S PROMISE.

Wishing you the best of blessings,

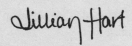

QUESTIONS FOR DISCUSSION

1. At the beginning of the story, how would you describe Justin's character? What are his weaknesses and strengths? What are his issues?

2. What is Rori's reaction when she first sees Justin in town? What does this tell you about her character? What are her issues?

3. In the beginning of the story Rori wrestles with regrets. She wants to go back in time and do over parts of her life. Have you ever felt this way? How has it affected you and how have you handled it?

4. Why does Justin decide to let Rori interview for the job? What does this say about him?

5. What role does the past play in the story? How does it support both Justin's and Rori's faiths? How does it develop and renew their romance?

6. Why is it painful for Justin to be around Rori? How does this change throughout the story? Why does it change?

7. What are the central themes? How do they develop? What meanings do you find in them?

8. How does God guide both Justin and Rori through their pain and fears?

9. Rori fears that men do not love deeply the way women do, and she fears she will wind up alone. How is this challenged through the book? What causes her to change? What does she learn about love and regrets?

10. What role do the animals play in the story?

11. What happens to make Rori let go of the past? How does she find self-forgiveness and understanding?

12. What do you like most about Rori and Justin as a couple? How do you know they are meant for each other?

13. How would you describe Frank and Cady's romance? What fears keep them apart?

14. Why does Justin finally take down his guard and open his heart to love? What makes him believe in true love again? What does he learn about love and life?

Love Inspired

TITLES AVAILABLE NEXT MONTH

Available June 29, 2010

THE GUARDIAN'S HONOR
The Bodine Family
Marta Perry

KLONDIKE HERO
Alaskan Bride Rush
Jillian Hart

HEART OF A COWBOY
Helping Hands Homeschooling
Margaret Daley

CATTLEMAN'S COURTSHIP
Carolyne Aarsen

WAITING OUT THE STORM
Ruth Logan Herne

BRIDE IN TRAINING
Gail Gaymer Martin

HARLEQUIN®

A Romance

FOR EVERY MOOD™

Spotlight on
Heart & Home

Heartwarming romances
where love can happen
right when you least expect it.

See the next page to enjoy a sneak peek
from Silhouette Special Edition®,
a Heart and Home series.

*Introducing McFARLANE'S PERFECT BRIDE
by* USA TODAY *bestselling author Christine Rimmer,
from Silhouette Special Edition®.*

Entranced. Captivated. Enchanted.

Connor sat across the table from Tori Jones and couldn't help thinking that those words exactly described what effect the small-town schoolteacher had on him. He might as well stop trying to tell himself he wasn't interested. He was powerfully drawn to her.

Clearly, he should have dated more when he was younger.

There had been a couple of other women since Jennifer had walked out on him. But he had never been entranced. Or captivated. Or enchanted.

Until now.

He wanted her—*her,* Tori Jones, in particular. Not just someone suitably attractive and well-bred, as Jennifer had been. Not just someone sophisticated, sexually exciting and discreet, which pretty much described the two women he'd dated after his marriage crashed and burned.

It came to him that he…he *liked* this woman. And that was new to him. He liked her quick wit, her wisdom and her big heart. He liked the passion in her voice when she talked about things she believed in.

He liked *her.* And suddenly it mattered all out of proportion that she might like him, too.

Was he losing it? He couldn't help but wonder. Was he cracking under the strain—of the soured economy, the McFarlane House setbacks, his divorce, the scary changes in his son? Of the changes he'd decided he needed to make in his life and himself?

Strangely, right then, on his first date with Tori Jones, he didn't care if he just might be going over the edge. He was having a great time—having *fun*, of all things—and he didn't want it to end.

Is Connor finally able to admit his feelings to Tori, and are they reciprocated?
Find out in MCFARLANE'S PERFECT BRIDE
by USA TODAY bestselling author Christine Rimmer.
Available July 2010,
only from Silhouette Special Edition®.

Love Inspired

Bestselling author

JILLIAN HART

launches a brand-new continuity

ALASKAN *Bride* RUSH

*Women are flocking to the land of the Midnight Sun
with marriage on their minds.*

A tiny town full of churchgoing, marriage-minded men? For
Karenna Digby Treasure Creek sounds like a dream come true.
Until she's stranded at the ranch of search-and-rescue guide
Gage Parker, who is *not* looking for love. But can she *guide* her
Klondike hero on the greatest adventure of all—love?

KLONDIKE HERO

*Available in July
wherever books are sold.*

Steeple
Hill®

LI87608

www.SteepleHill.com